# *Believe*

"All the world is made of faith, and trust, and pixie dust."

— J.M. Barrie, *Peter Pan*

# *Believe*

Julie Mathison

Starr Creek Press

ISBN: 978-1-7350037-0-2 (Paperback)
ISBN: 978-1-7350037-2-6 (Hardback)
ISBN: 978-1-7350037-1-9 (eBook)

Library of Congress Control Number: 2020908210



Front cover design by Robin Vuchnich.
Star graphics by Korenyugin52.

Starr Creek Press, LLC
P.O. Box 212
Corvallis, OR, 97333

www.juliemathison.com

*For my parents, Dan and Mary, who taught me everything worth knowing.*

# CONTENTS

## ONE
# *Angels and Demons*

The first time I met Sabrina, she came out of nowhere.

*March 18, 1980*, I'd just written in my notebook. I like to document my entries for future reference. *Does time exist in heaven?*

I was sitting in the tube, just like I did every recess, just minding my own business. This question had been bugging me for a while now, and I was mulling it over, chewing on the nub of my pen, when who should come sauntering up but Karen and Kim, with Leanne straggling behind like she didn't know what they were up to.

And maybe she didn't, I don't know. She has a face that's hard to read.

Karen slapped on the concrete with her palm a few times. "Yoo hoo, anybody home?"

That started Kim laughing, like this was the funniest thing in the history of the world. Sometimes I think Kim doesn't have much going on upstairs, if you know what I mean.

"What are you doing in your little hidey-hole, Smell-an-ie?" Karen said in a sing-song voice.

I was curled up with my notebook against my knees, like you have to be when you sit in the tube, which is just a big piece of culvert, all on its own.

"Maybe she's a mute," Kim said, as if she half believed it, as if she hadn't heard me say, "here," every day in Miss Gorman's class, even if that's about all I said. Karen must have thought that was pretty dumb too, because she gave Kim a bug-eyed look that said so. When you're bullying people around, it's a real hassle to look like a moron.

"I'll make her talk," Karen said, and Kim laughed again, pinched and high.

I tried to picture Karen in her underpants, which I heard once was supposed to give you confidence, but frankly, that made her seem even more scary. So I looked past her to the trees in the empty lot, their leaves flipping over in the wind, all shivery and bright. I could almost feel the wind on my face, almost drift away completely—except that the knot in my stomach wouldn't let go.

"Here." Karen made a lunge for my notebook. "Let's see what you're always scribbling."

"Come on, Karen," Leanne said in a wispy voice. I had forgotten she was there. "Let's do some penny drops."

"In a minute. Come on, Smellanie. Have you been writing about me?" And she lunged again, so I tucked the notebook into my chest and flipped onto my side, just like a stop-drop-and-roll fire drill.

That's when I ran smack into Sabrina.

She was sitting beside me, and the weirdest thing was, she looked just like Sabrina Duncan. She's my favorite Charlie's Angel. I guess it's a dumb show, what with bombs exploding and people getting kidnapped all the time or trapped in abandoned wells. But if I ever found myself the victim of an international espionage plot, I'd want Sabrina by my side.

"Why don't you tell her your name is *Melanie*?" she suggested. "And while you're at it, tell her that her fly is open."

And that's just what I did. Karen looked down at her brand-spanking-new designer jeans. Then, I thought her head would explode. I'll have to remember how she looked the next time I'm trying to visualize myself out of a scrape.

After that, Sabrina and I were inseparable.

"Do you ever watch *Charlie's Angels*?" I asked her a few days later.

Sabrina isn't her real name, by the way. I had been waiting to ask her about *Charlie's Angels* because I wasn't sure she'd like someone telling her she looked like a pint-sized Kate Jackson knock-off with her brown eyes and black hair. I mean, maybe her favorite angel was Kelly or Kris, or even Jill. But I should have known better.

"Sure," she said. "Kind of a dopey show, except for Sabrina."

That got me excited, like we were sharing the same brain.

"Exactly," I whispered. We were talking in the back of science class and I didn't want to get in trouble. "Has anyone ever told you that you look like her? If Sabrina was a kid."

Sabrina-to-be got a devilish look in her eye. "Let's pretend I *am* her," she said. "Why not? Call me Sabrina from now on."

That's when I knew we were soul mates. I also like to imagine things just so. Only I'm not very good at living them that way.

"Check it out," Colin said to no one in particular. He and Davis were eating their pop rocks instead of putting them in the soda bottle, where they were supposed to have a chemical reaction. "Look, I'm going to explode." And he pretended to take a big swig of Coke.

"Ohhh nooooooo!" Davis said in his high, whiny Mr. Bill voice. "My body is groooowing!" he crooned, holding his belly with both hands, then clutching his hair. "My head is the size of a big balloooon!"

Colin jumped in as the narrator, Mr. Hands, and explained how Mr. Bill's remains would be a boon to science. I saw an episode of Mr. Bill on *Saturday Night Live* once when Dad was asleep, but Colin and Davis must watch it all the time. They go through at least one of these routines every day: how poor little Claymation Bill, with his white face and mouth like a red Cheerio, meets a grisly end.

"Here, let me help reform you into a brain-eating amoeba," Colin was saying, in his role as Mr. Hands, smushing Davis around like a ball of clay.

"Don't forget to wash your *hands*!" Sabrina chimed in, which was corny, but funny too, because teachers are always sending Colin and Davis off to the bathroom to do just that. They have questionable judgment.

It felt good to be a part of things. I used to wish I had a friend the way Colin and Davis are friends, even though they live in their own universe and no one pays them any mind.

But now, I have Sabrina.

***

Buckminster Experimental School is nothing like the school I used to go to, where we sat at the same desk all day and called the teachers Mr. This and Mrs. That. Here, I'm supposed to call my teachers by their first names to encourage a sense of fraternity. But I never do. Luckily, I don't talk much, so no one notices.

The people who built the school named it after R. Buckminster Fuller, a very old, forward-thinking man who talked about ecology before it was something they put on lunchboxes. They wanted to build a geodesic dome because that was Mr. Fuller's big idea, but I guess they ran out of money for that, because our school is just in one hallway of a regular school. We mosey up and down the hall all day long, going to our different classes.

My favorite teacher is Miss Gorman. Laurelann. She teaches English, and I *loooove* English. If I could read books all the time, that's just what I'd do. When I come home from the Fairview Public Library with an armload of books, I lay them all out on the living room floor and try to decide which to read first. Each one is like a shimmering orb of possibility, especially when they're all there, side by side. I was going to say that reading a book is like going on a trip to a fantastical place, but it just occurred to me that the way I mostly feel is that I'm home after having been away a long time.

I was sitting in Miss Gorman's class, about three weeks after I met Sabrina, when everything changed.

"Who here has read *Peter Pan*?"

I was dying to raise my hand. Sabrina kicked me with the side of her shoe. Of course, no one else had read it, so Miss Gorman went on, never knowing how much we had in common.

"Listen, kids," she said, in that way she has of talking like she's in your living room, "I was thinking we might try our hand at staging a production. What do you think?"

What did I *think*? I could already see myself zipping across the stage on wires in my little green suit! Sabrina kicked my foot again and made this sound in the back of her throat, like she had popcorn stuck in it.

Luckily, the other kids were as excited as I was. Pretty soon, Miss Gorman was back with a pile of papers.

"Raise your hand if you'd like an audition form."

I don't know what it is about me, really I don't. I get right up to the edge of things, but I can't jump, like my feet are glued to the ground, like maybe there's a long fall on the other side that goes down and down forever. Sabrina was clearing her throat for all she was worth, kicking away, and Miss Gorman was already walking the aisles, handing those papers out, one by one. Any minute, she would walk right by, and there I'd still be, sitting and waiting for who knows what.

That's when Sabrina reached over to fling my arm up, like I was an extra in *Zombie's Revenge*.

"Melanie," Miss Gorman said, and her face turned on with a soft, white light. "I'm so glad you'll be participating."

And I could tell she meant it. That day, even going home to Dad couldn't bring me down.

TWO

# *Ghosts*

Dad looks like a faun that lost its horns and hooves. He's got big brown eyes and wavy hair that women must have been gaga about back in the day because, to hear Mom tell it, she snatched him up. They used to joke about that a lot, who snatched who up, like they were competitors in some kind of Supermarket Bonanza Spree.

I was feeling so good with that audition sheet hot in my hands that I plucked up the nerve to ask Sabrina over after school.

"Sure," she said. "I'd love to meet your dad," even though I couldn't remember telling her about him. Sometimes, when I get going, I don't even know what comes out of my mouth.

We headed down First Avenue through the downtown part of Fairview, with all its little ragtag stores. Fairview got left behind when the freeway was built, and now you only come here if you mean to, but you can tell it used to be on the main drag. There's the Woolworth's and the menswear store and the movie theater. The old J. C. Penney building is still there, but they moved out to the mall last year, so now it looks lonely with those big windows full of nothing but sky. Everything in Fairview is old, which suits me fine.

"Do you like old houses?" I asked Sabrina.

She thought about it, flipping her hair off her face with a toss of her head. She's got this way of squinting off into the distance like she might be plotting a big rescue operation.

"Sure, why not," she said, which was a letdown since I was expecting something more.

You see, I have this theory that houses that have been around for a long time—for years or decades, or even centuries—remember what they've seen. You can feel it when you walk in, all those memories settled in like ghosts with nothing better to do than jaw about the old days. I love that feeling. An old house belongs in the way that a new house never will—until it gets old. But, somehow, they don't build houses that collect ghosts anymore.

We turned onto Rosemary Street, which is perfect, like my house. There we stood at the top of the weedy front walk, gazing up at its creaky, Victorian goodness. Sure, the red paint is chipped, and the wisteria looks like it's trying to eat the house, but I get goosebumps every time I come home.

"My dad's kind of . . . different," I said.

"Different *how*?"

I couldn't find the right words, so I just said, "You'll see," and led the way to the front stairs.

We walked in to find him exactly where I knew we would, in his corner of the big front room.

"Why is the music so loud?" Sabrina mouthed over the twangs of guitar coming out of the stereo.

I hustled over to turn down the knob, but then the song was over anyway, and there was only the hiss and click of the record needle settling back into its cradle.

In the silence, I cleared my throat. "Hi Dad," I said, then, just as an experiment, "I brought someone home today. Hope that's okay."

Sure enough, he was really deep in. He had his paint brush held in his fingers like a scalpel, like he was a surgeon in the final stages of a life-and-death operation. Sometimes he uses the big brush, and then it's all swooshes and swirls, using his whole arm because the canvas is huge, the size of the wall. But today, I could see he'd entered a black hole. He was working on some itty-bitty galaxy that had caught his eye and was long gone.

"That's great, Moo Moo," he said, from a long way off. "Snack's in the fridge."

"My friend's name is Sabrina," I tried.

"Mmm hmm," he said. He squinted and turned his head, peering into the painting as if he'd seen something new.

I yanked my head toward the kitchen, and Sabrina followed me down the hall to the back of the house.

"At least he makes you a snack."

"Oh, yeah, he always does." I shrugged like it was no big deal, but Sabrina seemed to know.

"My Dad works all day long at an explosives factory, so I never see him either."

We both laughed because I knew she was just trying to make me feel better.

"Does he bring cool stuff home?"

We giggled a little as we got an armload of goodies from the fridge to take up to my room—the ham sandwich my dad had made and some orange juice and apple sauce. Mom doesn't believe in junk food, so we still don't keep it around the house.

We walked up the narrow, dark staircase to the second floor. I should have known better than to start thinking about Mom. It's like poison gas that seeps out.

Sabrina kicked the door closed behind her and put her load on the dresser. Sure enough, she said, "So, what about your Mom?" like she'd picked up the scent.

Oh boy, here we go.

"She's traveling. For work," I said and hoped that was that. Mom and I used to sit for hours in the window seat, snuggling and pointing at pictures in *National Geographic*. We'd dream about all the exotic people she would interview, the articles she'd write about life on the African savanna or in the slums of Beirut. "She's, you know, here and there."

"Traveling abroad," Sabrina said, with a nod. "You're in touch?"

"Oh, yeah, of course. I write postcards all the time." But I guess my mouth wasn't done talking because, out of the blue, it said, "It was Mom who read *Peter Pan* to me, when I was just a little kid. Neverland was our secret place."

"Perfect," Sabrina said, like she hadn't even noticed my bunched-up voice. "So when you get the part of Peter Pan, you can write her all about it."

My eyes popped wide. "How did you know?" I hadn't told anyone how much I wanted the lead.

Sabrina just waved me off. "Reading people is what I do."

Maybe that's what made up my mind to spill the beans. I read people too, even though sometimes I get the pages mixed up.

"The truth is she disappeared last year." I sank down on the bed beside her. That must have been a lot to digest, even for someone like Sabrina, so we just sat there for a minute or two.

"You mean you really don't know where she is?" she said, quietly, like it was a secret.

I shrugged. "I used to pretend she was in Istanbul," and I went on to describe an exceptionally chilling escape from the Turkish authorities.

But Sabrina wasn't interested.

"I'll tell you what," she said. "You need to find out where she *really* is. Adults are useless at these things." And she was right, because Dad and Gloria and Roxie and Roland had all given up, like Mom was just gone, like she had meant to go.

But I knew that couldn't be true.

*"Now,* you're thinking," Sabrina said, catching the gleam in my eye. "What do adults know anyways? They've been standing in line so long, they don't even remember what for."

Then, Sabrina went on to tell me about *her* parents.

"You mean, your dad really *does* work in an explosives factory?" I said, laughing.

"Only as part of his cover," she said with a wink. I thought that was brilliant because of the whole *Charlie's Angels* look-alike thing.

"How late can you stay?" Now that I was thinking about *Charlie's Angels*, I thought maybe we could watch a rerun together. I could feel Dad downstairs, as if his own little world had swallowed up the whole house, and it all felt so lonely.

"As late as you want," she said, and flopped back on my bed with her arms wide.

I guess Sabrina is just about the ideal friend.

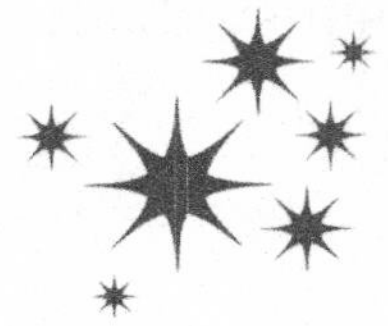

# THREE
## *Building Houses*

If you've never seen *Charlie's Angels*, it's a show about a crime-fighting trio of ladies who work for a private detective agency. At the beginning of every show, they get a call on the speakerphone from their boss, Charlie, who tells them about the case and then sends them on their way. They might be off to some high-security military installation in the desert, or to a fancy hotel where they have to pose as heiresses in order to uncover a kidnapping plot, or whatever. At the end, after some tight scrapes, they always get together on the phone again and laugh about it, like it was no big deal. They never actually *meet* Charlie, only sometimes we see him from the back with a bunch of ladies on his arm.

Like I said, it's a dumb show. How come they have an invisible man for a boss? If I were to make it up,

Sabrina would be her own boss. Actually, she could be the boss of the other two because they need a little looking after. But I like to watch it anyway, and besides, life is full of things that don't make sense.

"Why do you think Peter Pan lives in Neverland?" I asked Sabrina while we were sitting in wood shop, working on our bird house. "I mean, why name it *that*?"

"Because it's where you never grow up," Sabrina said, sensibly. But I was going deeper.

"Sure, but why not call it *Ever*land, or *Forever*land? You know, to emphasize that it's a place where you *always* get to be a kid?"

These things had never occurred to me back in the days when Mom and I would make blanket forts at my old house, pretending to be lost boys, hiding from Captain Hook.

Sabrina shrugged and glued another piece of birch bark to the roof. Our birdhouse was going to be the most amazing one ever, with two stories for sociability and pretty little eaves.

"Because it's written by an adult?" she said. That sounded sensible too. It would be just like an adult to take a wonderful idea and miss the whole point. Maybe it was because Mr. Barrie couldn't remember what it was like to be a kid, not really, like it was an island he left behind ages ago and could no longer find on a map.

"Ooh, Smellanie is making a bird's nest," Karen said, breezing by with her project on a tray. I had to admit, her jewelry box was pretty good. "And it looks just like a bird made it, too. How authentic." She must have learned that word recently, because she'd been showing it off every chance she got.

"Why, thank you," Sabrina said, brightly. "Cheer up, Karen. It just takes some people a little longer to master basic motor skills."

Karen tossed her hair and headed past to sit down at her table with Kim and Leanne. Sabrina shot me a look, and I stifled a giggle.

"Don't feel bad," she whispered to me. "I mean, she treats me like I'm invisible. Have you ever heard her say a *word* to me?"

"Yeah, but that makes you lucky," I said. "Besides, she only ignores you because you picked me over her."

It makes me feel good that Sabrina sat in the tube with me that fateful day. Our die was cast.

Mr. Olford wandered up with his big, stained coffee mug in his big, stained hand and looked down at what we had going on. He likes to rest his arm on top of his belly, like it's a table.

"Hmmm, good," he said, nodding approvingly. He's a man of few words, but I can see he likes to talk with his eyes. I think a lot of people miss that about him. He's the only teacher who goes by his last name because he doesn't like his first. No one even knows what it is, but I've heard some not-so-nice guesses floating around.

Quiet people get a bum rap.

"And here is where the perch is going to go," I said, holding up the little dowel under one of the holes. I'd been talking more in my classes lately.

"Hmmm, yes." he said, turning his head the other way and looking straight into my eyes.

After shop class, Sabrina and I had math with Mr. Funkel and then guitar, which is one of our electives. On sign up day, they post sheets for the different classes all down the hallway and release the students in groups to write their names in. It can be dicey, trying to get the ones you want, especially when you've got a friend to think about. Sabrina and I got the very last slots in guitar.

"Who do you think will be trying out for the play?" I whispered to Sabrina as we tuned our guitars. We were all sitting in a circle on pillows in the middle of the room, with the desks pushed off to the sides. The class is small because there are only eight guitars.

"I saw Karen's hand go up," Sabrina said.

"Yeah, me too." I was on pins and needles because the audition was coming up, right after school. "Maybe she'll get sick with some disgusting illness at lunch."

"It's past lunchtime," Sabrina pointed out. "But these things can take time to develop. Look for signs of a rash."

My favorite thing about guitar is that neither Karen nor Kim are in it. Leanne is, though, and she usually sits next to David, saying nothing, even though she's always looking at him on the sly. David has brown, feathery hair and tannish skin, and he looks like he belongs in a Mountain Dew commercial, swinging out over a lake on a tire swing. He keeps one of those combs with the big handle in his back pocket, and every now and again he'll run it through his glorious locks, shaking his head out, like it's all happening in slow motion. Most of the fifth-grade girls seem to think he's a dreamboat.

"Why won't the G chord work!" Tammy said. Mrs. Brandy got up, holding the neck of her guitar in one hand, and went over to sit between the twins, Tammy and Tory, who are the only fourth graders in the class. The rest of us kept plugging through the first few bars of *Leaving on a Jet Plane*.

"What's her story?" Sabrina whispered, leaning over and casting her steely gaze on Leanne, who was struggling too, moving her hand up and down the frets, trying to find the right place to press the strings down. She shook out her hand, then stuck a couple of fingers in her mouth. I know how that feels, until you build up callouses. The truth is, right now, she looked kind of harmless and cute.

"I can't figure her out," I said, which is saying something because I have a sixth sense about people that rarely lets me down. I'm like a dog that can sniff out fear, only I'm attuned to a person's soul and whether it's benign or malignant. Those are words doctors use to describe tumors, but I think it suits souls just fine because everyone has a story, even people like Karen. She probably has a mean dad or bossy siblings, although every once in a while you hear about a kid who starts pulling the wings off butterflies straight out of the cradle. I wonder about that, really I do. "She's quiet, like me," I said, finally.

"But *why*," Sabrina said, unconvinced. "Because she's shy or because she thinks she's above everybody else?"

Just then, Colin burst into the room and said, "Oh, I thought this was the bathroom!" then shut the door again and went off down the hall, laughing his head off. I don't know anyone better at amusing themselves than Colin and Davis.

Finally, there was nothing left between me and the end of the day, and we headed for homeroom. Miss Gorman is the fifth-grade homeroom teacher, so the plan was that everyone who wanted to audition would just stay behind after the bell. I felt like I had to pee. I told Sabrina I'd catch up, but then nothing came out, so I just washed my hands for about five minutes, staring at my face in the mirror, warped and dingy, because the mirror is just a big piece of stainless steel.

"What *took* you so long?" Sabrina said as I slipped into my seat. Miss Gorman was already talking. I could see Kim and Karen whispering in the corner, Kim's hair flapping around her face like a couple of dog ears. She wears it every day the same way, in two long, tubular curls, which makes her face look like a hot dog sandwiched between two buns. They were looking our way and giggling.

"Now, class, remember," Miss Gorman was saying, "I really want you to put it out there. Let us see everything you've got. Don't hold back." And she went on like that for a while, cheering us on to bare our souls to the general population. I could already feel my cheeks getting red. Any minute we'd head over to the auditorium, and then my doom would be sealed.

I thought I was going to throw up.

# FOUR
# *Pixie Dust*

I thought I had to pee again, so by the time I arrived at the auditorium, everyone was seated in the first two rows, and Miss Gorman was up in front, giving her spiel. I must have been in such a scramble, I didn't even look for Sabrina but just slipped into a seat a few rows back, thinking no one would notice me if I changed my mind about walking the last mile. "Walking the last mile" is what convicts do when they're headed for the chair, Old Sparky, then on to meet their maker, and that's pretty much how I felt.

"So, without further ado," Miss Gorman said, picking up the first form in her pile and flipping her glasses onto her nose, "Karen, you're up. Let's see what you've got."

Of course, Karen was sitting closest to the stage stairs, raring to go. She walked up with her head high, like she was already hearing applause in there, echoing all over the place, what with her having such a big head and small brain. I shouldn't say things like that, but sometimes I do write them down in my notebook, which is what I was doing now. She belted out a pretty good rendition of *You Light Up My Life*, although it lacked pathos. Then, she rattled off some of Tiger Lily's lines, and some of Wendy's and the mother's, and even Tinkerbell's. I guess she was casting her net widely.

"That will do, Karen. Thank you so much," Miss Gorman said.

Next up were a few fourth graders, whom I pegged as decent mermaids and lost boys, and then Harry Fowler, who has a squarish head and always speaks as if he doesn't quite trust the syllables coming out of his mouth. I decided if Harry Fowler could do this, surely I could. I was even beginning to enjoy myself and felt like I should call for popcorn. Then, things really got going with Colin and Davis, who insisted on auditioning together.

"Boys, if you could stick to the script, just for now," Miss Gorman said. "I'm sure we'll be putting those improvisational skills to good use when we get to rehearsals." She should get a medal for tact, which has got to be as hard as dragging bodies off a battlefield, at least when it comes to Colin and Davis.

"Fie, dragon spawn! Unhand that maiden or I will smite thy head from thy body like a ripe pumpkin!"

Davis gave a chilling, evil laugh and dragged the mop he was holding hostage backwards across the stage. "Fat chance, muesli muncher! She is destined for the orc pits where I will soon build my engines of universal destruction!"

They had started out as pirates but by now had veered pretty far off-script. It sounded to me like a mash-up of Dungeons and Dragons and *Lord of the Rings* with some choice Nordic insults thrown in, and I was just dying to hear what came next, but I guess Miss Gorman had to keep things on track.

"Excellent, boys. I know just where to put you," she called out over the clatter of the mop bucket going over. "And next we have . . . Melanie Harper. Melanie?" She turned around. "Melanie, are you here?"

The minute I heard my name, my brain went kaput. I felt my face go white, and for a minute I just sat there, and sat and sat until everyone in the first two rows had turned around and was looking straight at me. Then, my body kicked in, and I felt it stand up and walk me down the aisle and up the stairs, just like I was on a conveyor belt, ready to be boxed and shipped off to a Kroger's supermarket.

"And what have you prepared for us today?" Miss Gorman said. She spoke slowly, and I could feel the worry in her eyes, even though I couldn't see them in the dimness of the space. The worry just made me more nervous because I could see now that I was going to let her down too, and that was worse than just being a chicken the whole time, thinking you weren't going to be and then going off at the last minute, all feathers and squawking. "Would you like to sing something?" she said.

"Yes," I cleared my throat. "Yes, ma'am."

"Laurelann," she reminded me. "Call me Laurelann. And what will you sing?"

I had prepared *The Rose* in the shower, but in my current state, I thought it best to play it safe.

"Can I just sing *Twinkle, Twinkle*?"

I could hear Karen snickering with Kim beside her, but Miss Gorman just put this warm smile into her voice and said, "What you sing doesn't matter, sweetheart. Just put your heart into it."

The *sweetheart* bit helped a little. She'd never called me that before. I could tell even Karen heard it because she stopped snickering and started sulking.

"Twinkle, twinkle, little star," I started out, unsteady, but on key. I have a fantastic voice in the shower, but it might just be the acoustics, what with the shower curtain and all that steam helping your voice billow up and grow. Up here on the stage, it sounded lost and reedy. I had this sinking feeling that I was going to walk down those stairs in a few minutes without Miss Gorman ever knowing what I could do.

"That was excellent, Melanie. Now, how about some lines."

I had only practiced lines for Peter Pan because I didn't want any other part, but now it seemed like I was full of myself. Who was I to get the lead role? I knew that's what Karen would think, and Kim would think it because Karen told her to, and so I was shuffling my feet and stalling, gazing out at all those empty seats and wishing I'd see a friendly face when—suddenly, I did.

Sabrina was out there after all! She was in the very back row, where no one could see her but me, and she was pulling all kinds of pranks, grabbing her own neck with both hands and pretending to choke herself down out of sight behind the chairs, then popping up to drag herself with one arm by the neck all the way down the row. She'd fall over and I'd see a leg go up, then she'd struggle up over the chair back as if locked in a to-the-death battle with herself. That's when I laughed because, all of a sudden, I could see her point. That was me, alright. I was my own worst enemy. And it occurred to me, like a blast of fresh air out of nowhere, that I didn't have anything to lose.

"I'll teach you how to jump on the wind's back and then away we go," I began, diving into the nursery scene, and I could feel a thrill go right through me.

Miss Gorman thumbed through her script, filling in for Wendy and John as I tempted them off to Neverland and taught them how to fly. At first, it was like being back in that blanket fort with Mom, with only the two of us in the whole wide world. But then, with each line, more pieces of the dark, hushed auditorium began to fall away. No one was whispering now, not even the second graders who had snuck in to watch, and there we all were, *together*, with old-fashioned cradles and hobby horses strewn about, and Wendy's canopied bed in the corner, and the tall, dormer windows thrown open to the night sky.

"You just think lovely, wonderful thoughts, and they lift you up in the air," I breathed, and as I spoke, the words did just that, lifted me up so that I sailed across the stage, thinking about nothing at all but that sky full of stars and how long eternity must be.

"Oh, Melanie," Miss Gorman said when I came down to earth, all flushed and breathless because I couldn't believe what had just happened. "That was really marvelous. *Thank* you."

Karen gave me the evil eye as I came down the stairs, but I couldn't wipe that grin off my face to save my life. I went back and got my notebook, and then Sabrina came and sat by me for the rest of the audition.

"You nailed it!" she said proudly. I told her I couldn't have done it without her. "Well, if I can decide to be Sabrina Duncan, then I guess you can decide to be whatever you want," she said.

And I thought, for a split second, maybe she was right, maybe make-believe was as good as the real thing when you could share it with the world. But I still wasn't sure. I would have to wait and see.

"Thanks for showing up," I said, and then we held hands for the rest of the hour.

# FIVE
# *The Princess and the Pea*

When the cast list came out, you could have bowled me over with a feather.

Miss Gorman posted it outside the homeroom door in between fourth and fifth periods. And there was my name at the top of the list.

*Peter Pan: Melanie Harper.*

I'd been waiting three days to see those words, but it felt like I'd been waiting my whole life.

"Avast, ye bilge rat! Look alive, or I'll take ye for a floater!"

Colin had been cast as Captain Hook and Davis as Smee, Hook's right-hand pirate, so to speak. They wasted no time in exploring their roles.

"Har, ye scurvy knave! I'll run yer liver up the flagpole afore I lets ye speak to me that way!"

And off they went down the hall, using their binders as makeshift bludgeons.

But I hardly noticed them.

Me. Peter Pan.

I must have stood there, just gaping and staring, for about ten minutes. People kept coming up to look over my shoulder, and a few of them gave me a pat on the arm and said things like, "Good job," and "See you at rehearsal."

Sabrina snapped me out of it.

"Did you see who got the part of Wendy?"

Indeed, I had. Karen. What could Miss Gorman be thinking? She probably had a secret plan to make Karen a nicer person in spite of herself. It would be just like Miss Gorman to think that way, but I knew it would take more than a little white nightgown to turn Karen around. We're talking serious pixie dust.

"It'll be okay," I said, determined to enjoy my moment.

The rest of the list seemed about right with Rachel Bell as Tiger Lily, Harry Fowler as Mr. Darling and the crocodile, and the twins, Tammy and Tory, cast jointly as Tinker Bell, in case either one of them got tired. There were a lot of minor parts too, lost boys and pirates, mermaids and Indians, so everyone had a role.

Even Leanne was on the list. She hadn't tried out, but I guess Miss Gorman must have talked to her because there was her name at the very bottom.

*Stage Manager: Leanne Smith.*

The stage manager is the person who gets to boss everyone around backstage. I couldn't imagine Leanne doing that. But she is kind of stern, because she hardly ever smiles, so that should keep people in line. I saw her next to me, looking at the cast list for about two minutes, and I just got this *feeling*, like she wanted to talk to me. I've caught her staring a couple of times in class lately, and I thought maybe she'd seen the auditions after all, which was kind of a nice feeling. But then, I got worried that I was getting a big head, just like Karen, so I reeled it in. I probably just have hairs sticking out of my nose, and that's what she finds so interesting.

"Hey look!" Sabrina said, pointing to the bottom of the page. "I'm a stage hand!"

Good old Miss Gorman. She never leaves anyone out.

I could hardly wait to get home and tell Dad. Even if he didn't hear a word I said, still, I'd get to stand there in the living room and say those sweet words, "Dad, I got the part!"

But when I got home, he wasn't there.

"Dad!" I yelled, walking around from room to room. I was just thinking he'd gone out for groceries when I heard some talking in the side yard.

"Well, well, if it isn't the Princess Pea," Roland said as I came around the walk and crossed under the bower. Roland is one of Dad's best friends, and he's known me ever since I was a baby. The story goes that I complained about a lumpy mattress when I was a toddler, after Mom read me a book of fairy tales. Some things, you never live down.

"Hey Moo Moo," Dad said, sitting in his favorite lawn chair, under the wisteria. I *loooove* the side yard. It's tucked between the house and a high fence overrun with roses that must be as old as the house. It qualifies as a forgotten place even though we use it all the time. More about that later. "Come on and park it," he said, and patted his knees.

Dad's got a mellow, good humor which is just about always there when his head isn't stuck in a painting. *Just* about always, although he has a third gear too, which he shifts into when he doesn't want to talk about things. Unlike regular gears, this one makes it *harder* to get going. He would sometimes use that one on Mom, late at night when they thought I was asleep and would have "discussions." I've heard him use it on Gloria too, Mom's mom. But he never uses it on me.

I settled in and told him the good news, turning around in his lap. For a second, I thought he was going to cry.

"Peter Pan," he said, his faun eyes all misty. Dad knew all about Mom and me playing Neverland because it's hard to keep a blanket fort secret, especially when it's in the living room. "Aw, Moo Moo . . ."

"Princess Pea takes New York!" Roland said, to change the mood, and he wiped one hand across the sky like he was laying out a headline. He leaned over in his wheelchair to grab a can of beer from the cooler. "And they said she only knew how to knit."

Most of the things Roland says are obscure, maybe because he's a university professor. Half the time, I'm not sure if he's trying to be funny or not. But he's a nice guy, in a corny way, and I know he loves me. He revved his wheelchair up and back a few times, like he was about to take off from a starting line, and made an engine sound out of the corner of his mouth. He's so good with his chair, it's like a pair of legs. You would hardly know he's only been paralyzed for a few years.

Then, Roxie came around the corner, carrying a stack of Styrofoam containers.

"Taco night!" she said and shouldered off her bag.

"Roxie!" I leapt off Dad's lap to give her a hug, barely waiting until she fumbled the containers into Roland's hands.

"Hey, hey!" she said, laughing, then wrapped her arms around me like she wouldn't be anywhere else, not for love or money. I smelled the horses and hay on her jacket, and it was like summer all over again, with me riding on the back of the baler, watching those golden bundles tumble out behind, or stepping into that big barn all full of quiet, with the birds flapping through shafts of light, way up high.

She pulled away, holding me by the shoulders, and looked me square in the eye. "We need to get you out to the farm. Good grief, it's been ages!"

I could tell what she was thinking. The last time I'd visited the farm, Mom had been with us too.

But I shook that off, and Roxie passed around the tacos, ducking into the backyard to bring back two more chairs. I told her my good news, and we all talked and ate until I was stuffed.

Dad said, "Why don't we have some tunes?"

I shot my hand up to volunteer, just like I was in school, and hopped up to go inside. I put on a Leon Russell album and flung up the window that opens onto the side yard, cranking the volume, then hightailing it out before my ear drums split. There's this song that makes you feel like you're sitting in a rainstorm with the cars swooshing and whooshing by on the wet pavement, all lonesome and happy at the same time. Leon Russell has a folksy, twangy voice and lots of happy-sad songs, but the last song on side one is a hoot.

Roland wheeled over to me and reached out his hand. "Lady, will you dance?" he asked. We cleared some space among the chairs for our jig and off we went, swatting wisteria branches away and yelling, "*Yee haw!*" and basically having the time of our lives. Roland dances in his chair like nobody's business, popping wheelies and twirling around. When the song was over, I flopped down like a rag doll.

That's just about the time I would have hopped onto Mom's lap for a recharge.

Mothers have a secret source of energy, hidden somewhere in their body, though medical science has yet to discover it. The energy comes out in little waves that you can feel, warm and full of God or love or whatever it is that makes galaxies turn. In fact, I'm thinking there's a mother smack in the middle of every one of those galaxies in Dad's paintings, and maybe that's what he's looking for, because he misses her too.

I could see the gig was up. The poisonous gas was out, and everyone had gotten a whiff. Sometimes, when you get too happy you tip right over into sadness if you don't watch out.

"So, how are you *doing*?" Roxie asked Dad, leaning forward with her elbows on her knees. They were already starting to forget about me. They'd been friends with Dad since college, and sometimes they'd come by to check up on him because we all knew what was coming down the pike.

In a few weeks, it would be our one-year anniversary of life without Mom.

I could see Dad fixing to shift into third gear, but then he choked up and turned his face away, looking through the bower into the backyard at something no one else could see. I wanted to go to him, but there was that knot in my stomach again, the one that never lets me get away. Only now it wouldn't let me reach out either. My throat got all achy with mean words, things I would never say, not in a million years.

The needle on the record player was bumping along at the end of side one. I could hear it through the window. "I'm going inside," I announced to no one in particular.

Maybe I could call Sabrina.

SIX

# A Change in the Air

The next morning, I decided it was high time to start on Sabrina's idea. Operation Find Mom. Short, sweet, and to the point. It might all come to nothing, but at least it would take my mind off things. Dad was a basket case, and I was only holding up because I had Sabrina. I even knew where to start—the *Detroit Free Press*, which is where Mom used to work.

I lay in bed, watching the family of squirrels in the old oak tree outside my window, which is one of my favorite things to do. They run up and down the trunk all day, grabbing nuts in their handy little paws, circling around out of sight, then popping up on a branch as if to say, *ta da!* They're always busy, and you can see nothing ever gets them down. I can disappear for a good, long time just watching them until, all of a sudden, I'm ready for business too. One day, I got that feeling when it was barely light outside, so I rode my bike downtown and watched the stores open up, one by one. It's a special feeling, when you're up before the world.

But today was a school day, so I hopped out of bed and threw on some clothes, pulling a comb through my stringy hair. I wanted to write a postcard to Mom, even though I didn't know where to send it yet. So I sat down at my beat-up desk and took one of the cards from my stash in the top drawer. I have a whole slew of them from years of collecting, which is what comes of dreaming about far-off places, though it never occurred to me I'd be sending them to Mom. They say ignorance is bliss.

I wanted to come across as cheerful, so I started out with my big news about *Peter Pan*, telling her all about the audition, even the part where I almost chickened out. Of course, I told her about Sabrina and how good she was in a pinch. And I couldn't help throwing in a few choice details about Karen that were good for a chuckle.

By the time I got to school, I was almost late for the bell.

"Take out your notebooks, please," Mr. Howard said as I slipped into my seat. "We're going to talk about some difficult subjects today, so fasten your seatbelt."

Mr. Howard's first name is Matthew. He teaches health and history, and his classes are full of difficult subjects, like the time we saw two lungs in glass cases, side by side, one as pink and healthy as a baby pig, the other like black lace from a lifetime of smoking. Then there was the day we learned about PCP, or Angel Dust, which makes kids not much older than me jump off bridges because they think they can fly, and rubber cement, which kills your brain cells when you stick it into a brown paper bag and sniff it. What kind of a dummy does that? Probably the same one who came up with "ignorance is bliss."

Today, we were going to talk about Hitler.

Mr. Howard lectured for a while, and then we watched a movie called *The Twisted Cross*, full of actual footage from Hitler's big parades. It gave me a chill, seeing how angry he was up at the podium and how excited it made everyone feel, acres and acres of people, stretching off as far as the eye could see. Then the soldiers came through, marching straight-legged in lockstep, like they were all of one mind, which was chilling too because it occurred to me that from up high, where Hitler was, they probably didn't look like people at all, but like a river, cutting through that crowd that was just a bunch of blond head and hats for the people who didn't want their dark hair to show. It must be easy to forget about people when they're just the scenery, or at least that's what I told myself because I had to come up with some reason Hitler could do all those terrible things.

By second period, I was ready for a break.

"Water, please?" I said to Sabrina, as if I were on my last leg. She had slipped in late, just when I was starting to get that pit in my stomach.

"Recess," Sabrina said with relief as we headed out of class, and for once I was in agreement, although recess is my least favorite part of the day. It's the time when you can't forget that you don't have any friends, and everyone else knows it too. Now I have Sabrina, but it can still be lonely, just the two of us, especially with the other kids being so loud about their good time. So I was glad when Misty Jones invited us to join her on the monkey bars. It made for a nice change from the tube. I left my notebook by the edge of the bark mulch, keeping an eye on it in case Karen sauntered by.

It seemed like things were looking up, so I couldn't figure out why I had that pit in my stomach. At first I thought it was because of Hitler, but then I realized I was worried about the first rehearsal, coming up the very next day. Sometimes I have to listen really hard to learn about myself, which is strange since I live with myself all the time.

"Hey, Smellanie," Karen called out from across the playground where she was walking on the moon, arms out to the side as she balanced at the top. Everyone calls it the moon because of Colin and Davis, who like to space walk around it in slow motion, but it's just a big upside-down bowl made of crisscrossed bars. "I'll bet you think you're hot stuff since you got that part," she said, loud enough for everyone to hear. Kim started sniggering from where she was hanging down below, but then yelped and dropped down when Karen stepped on her fingers. "Watch out, you dope," Karen said, like it was her own fingers that had gotten squashed.

Sometimes I wonder why anyone is Karen's friend.

"The *lead* part," Sabrina said, but Karen was too busy grousing at Kim to hear. When she was done, she leapt off the moon, flapping her arms all goofy, like they were broken, and yelled, "Look at me, I can fly!" There were a few laughs here and there from kids who were only half watching. Most people tune Karen out.

"See you around," I said to Misty, then went to grab my notebook before Karen could nab it.

"Why do you let her talk to you that way?" Sabrina asked when we were safe in the tube.

I shrugged. "What am I supposed to say?"

Sabrina snatched the notebook out of my hands and flipped through. "How about this," she said, then started to read: "*Sometimes I wish Karen would move to another city, or maybe country, or maybe planet just so I'd have a chance.*" She snapped the notebook shut and handed it back. "You don't have trouble speaking your mind as long as you don't open your mouth."

I hunkered down and turned my head away.

"Do you think that's why you don't have any friends?" she asked. When I whipped my head back to look at her, she added, "I mean, other than me. Do you think if Karen wasn't here you'd be off rubbing elbows and hobnobbing like Dale Carnegie or something?"

Dale Carnegie was a public-speaking big shot back in olden times, which was funny, but I stifled my laugh.

"Maybe."

"You shouldn't lie to yourself," she said, which was hard to hear, even though her eyes were kind of soft and sorry. But I wasn't ready to stop being mad, so we just sat there saying nothing until the recess bell rang.

I thought about it all day. Why *was* it so hard for me to make friends? It had been hard even at my old school in Grayson, back in the good old days when

Mom was still around. Had books and blanket forts and Dad flipping pancakes behind his back *really* been enough? Or was I lying to myself, like Sabrina said? Because it wasn't like I hadn't noticed all those other kids, playing kick-the-can out in the street until way after dark.

By the time I plopped down in Miss Gorman's class, I was worn out, like I'd run a marathon in my head. David loped by, all easy, as if he was headed for a barbecue. Then Leanne sat down next to me. That was new. I looked over at Sabrina, on my other side. She cocked an eyebrow, but we still weren't talking.

"Alright, guys," Miss Gorman said. "I've decided to give you a chance to share your stories in class, with your peers. Any volunteers?"

Colin and Davis shot their arms up and started jiggling in their chairs, but Miss Gorman kept moving her head back and forth, looking for hands. I don't blame her. Personally, I enjoy their unique brand of creativity, but grown-ups can only take so many stories about the recently undead.

I didn't need to look at Sabrina to know what she was thinking. How hard could it be to raise my hand? What was wrong with me? How come my heart was yammering in my ears when all I was doing was thinking about it?

"Wonderful, Melanie! Your paper was one of my favorites."

I looked up. Sure enough, there was my hand, all on its own like a toddler that had wandered away from my body when I wasn't looking.

I cleared my throat and walked up to sit on the table under the blackboard. I cleared it again, staring at the paper she'd put into my hands. All I had to do was open my mouth, and then Sabrina would know I wasn't a complete basket case.

"The party of explorers," I began, my voice cracking. "The party of explorers had been lost for ten days in the jungle when the first man went missing."

"Whoa," Colin and Davis said as one.

I took this as a good sign and soldiered on. If I just thought about the words coming out of my mouth, it wasn't so bad, and the story was a real nail-biter. I was getting hooked all over again.

"They called him Lame Jerry on account of his bum leg, so at first his fellow explorers thought he must have fallen into a ravine, but the lone female member of their party knew better." I blushed a little, hoping no one would suspect that my character Jane Bravewell was a mash-up of Jane Goodall, that scientist who went to live with the apes, and, ahem, yours truly.

"Cannibals," Colin said, and Davis nodded gravely.

"Boys, please just listen," Miss Gorman said. I knew they wouldn't, though, and they were onto something, so I hurried on in case I got scooped.

Maybe it was the pressure of beating Colin and Davis to the punch, but the rest of the story just poured out.

"And when Jane, alone now for days since the last male explorer had vanished without a trace, looked up into the canopy of trees and saw the pygmy's face, she knew her doom was near, but not sealed. 'I'll make you a deal,' she said, having learned the pygmy language as a child when exploring with her parents. 'Release my fellow explorers and I will tell the bad men to stop burning your jungle home down.'" I had read about this in *National Geographic*, so I knew it was factually sound.

Colin and Davis stopped listening, now that they knew no one was going to be eaten, but I finished up the story to strong applause.

"Excellent, Melanie," Miss Gorman said, and quirked me a private smile. She probably just liked that my story had a moral, but it felt good all the same.

A few other kids read their papers too, and then the last bell rang. We were gathering up our books when I noticed Leanne and Miss Gorman talking at the front of class. Leanne kept looking over her shoulder at me. Then, they both walked over.

"Oh," I said, "hi." I felt my cheeks go red.

"Melanie," Miss Gorman put a hand on one of Leanne's shoulders, "I was wondering if you could help Leanne with her creative writing assignment, since you seem to have such a knack for it."

Leanne was looking anywhere but at me, but then our eyes met, and I realized for the first time how blue they were.

"Um, maybe you could come over to my house," she said in a careful voice. "Maybe Saturday."

It took a moment for this information to travel from Leanne's lips to my brain center, which was like a switchboard that had gone down from too many phone calls.

"Oh, you mean me," I said, like a dope, "come over to your house, sure." And I nodded a bunch of times to show I understood, even though my brain center was down. Miss Gorman had already walked back to her desk, leaving us to sort out the details.

"Can my parents pick you up?" Leanne asked, but I immediately switched to shaking my head no.

"Oh, no, no that's okay. I'll ride my bike. Just give me your address."

So she wrote it down, turned to go, and that was that.

"*Oh*, can I borrow your pen?" Sabrina said, when Leanne was gone, but I was too confused to even smile. I wasn't sure if Leanne liked the idea of me coming over to her house or not. Maybe it was all Miss Gorman's idea.

"Does this mean we're talking again?" I asked. We looked at each other, serious for a minute, until one or the other of us started us both giggling.

"Good story," Sabrina said. "So, when are we going to look for your mom?"

# SEVEN
# *Rummaging*

The *Detroit Free Press* has been in business since 1831 and even had correspondents on the battlefield during the Civil War. It has loads of Pulitzer Prizes to its name, and Mom felt really proud when they bought her first story. She wanted to be a regular correspondent which is why she worked undercover, trying to find out more about the Errol Flynns, a notorious Detroit gang.

"Seriously," I said, after I'd told Sabrina about it. "I wouldn't make this up."

She looked at me slant-eyed because, okay, I do make up stories sometimes. But she's one to talk. We're sort of like two criminals that way, Sabrina and I, thrown together by the very interest that drives us apart.

"She developed a whole network of contacts," I said. "People who used to be gang members or had family in the gang, or sometimes ones who wanted to get out."

Sabrina looked at me a moment longer, then said, "Well, it's not as dangerous as my dad's line of work, but at least she took it seriously."

A regular person might think that Sabrina was full of herself, but I happen to know she's kidding. She has a sideways sense of humor that most people don't catch.

I shrugged. "Anyway, I think it's a good place to start."

She screwed up her face so that her nose crinkled, the sort of perky thing her namesake would do. It was getting blustery out, and the wind whipped her straight dark hair around her face like she was driving in a convertible.

"So what are you saying?" she said. "That's she's been abducted or something?"

I bristled inside because I knew it sounded far-fetched, even pathetic. It was much more likely that Mom hadn't been in touch because she didn't want to be. That's what a reasonable person would think if they were confronted with the evidence in a court of law.

"Not abducted, exactly. I don't know. Maybe she decided to go deeper into her cover. Maybe she can't risk letting us know where she is, for our own safety."

Even to my ears, that sounded desperate, which is probably what softened Sabrina up.

"What am I giving you grief for," she said with a grin and threw her arm around my shoulder. "It's as good a theory as any. But what do we do about it?"

We were walking home from school, slowly, so we could talk it through.

"Maybe there's something in the attic."

The attic is where Dad had stowed all the stuff Mom left behind, all the scarves and letters and old perfumes we couldn't bear to part with when we moved from Grayson last year.

"Brilliant," Sabrina said, and I didn't even care if she was puffing me up. "No better time than the present."

Dad was out when we got home, so I didn't have to make up an excuse. The attic was dusty and musty, just the way an attic is supposed to be. If it wasn't for our mission, I might have brought up a good book. But we had work to do.

"Right," said Sabrina, rubbing her hands together. "I'll take that chest over there."

We worked quietly for a while with the wind kicking up outside the roof and throwing branches and green leaves against the window at the gable end. I thought a storm might be blowing in, and that made it even cozier there in the attic, and thrilling too, like being on an adventure without leaving the comfort of your home.

"Boy, she writes a lot," Sabrina said, plopping back onto her bottom to rifle through yet another accordion file. "Was she writing a novel?"

"Oh, yeah," I said, hopping up to go look over her shoulder. "It was about a female journalist caught up in the Six Day War in Israel." I could feel myself blushing, as if it were my book.

"Did you *read* it?"

I went back to the chest I'd been digging into. "Parts of it. Mom said some parts weren't child appropriate."

"Well, something *must* have happened to her, or else why would she just leave it behind?"

I didn't say anything because all of a sudden I had a lump in my throat. I'm sure Sabrina wasn't thinking about how the most important thing Mom had left behind was me.

"Of course," I managed finally. "It's just proof that she didn't know she'd be gone so long." I picked up the next bundle of dog-eared papers and thumbed through.

"Oh, like maybe she was going out on an undercover assignment that she couldn't even tell you and your dad about, only then it went wrong."

It sounded plausible, the way she said it. "Sure, only she must be okay because otherwise the police would have gotten involved." Now that Sabrina was on board, my idea seemed more and more realistic. I stopped flipping through pages and pulled one of the yellow, lined sheets out to peer more closely in the dim attic light. "Hey, I think I've got something here."

Sabrina was by my side in a flash. It was a list of names and addresses, scrawled in Mom's spidery handwriting.

"Some of those are Detroit addresses." Sabrina sounded impressed.

"I told you I wasn't making it up!" I said.

"Should we contact them? I know, maybe we can hitch a ride to Detroit. We can pretend we're on the lam from the police and we want to join up with the gang."

My stomach seized up, like I'd eaten an apple that was too green.

"Sure, maybe," I hedged. How on earth would we get to Detroit? Hitchhiking, like Sabrina said? "I'm not crazy about cars," I heard myself say, but Sabrina was already back at her trunk, looking for more clues.

She made a sound through her nose. "That's the least dangerous part of it," she said, but I figured that was false bravado. Just because Sabrina looks like a grown-up detective doesn't make her one.

I set the file down and turned back to the trunk, pushing aside a kimono that Mom had picked up in Little Tokyo when we visited Los Angeles years ago. I was just a baby, so I don't remember, but Mom talked so much about our trip out west that I have fake memories of it. Memory is a funny thing. After that, I found a copy of *Rebecca*, which Mom used to call her guilty pleasure, with the cover coming off at the seams. Tucked into the middle were a bunch of postcards she had collected, reminding me of the stash in my desk drawer.

I looked back at the list of addresses.

It was a long shot, but maybe I could try mailing a postcard to each address on the sheet. The worst thing that could happen was that someone would chuck it in the trash. Why not?

I was about to tell Sabrina my idea when I got interested in the papers behind the list, notes for a news story Mom must have been writing. Her writing was loose and loopy, just like I remembered, with lots of words crossed out and scribbles in the margins.

*The 1967 Detroit Riot, also known as the Twelfth Street Riot, lasted for five days, leaving 43 dead and 342 injured, and ushering in a decade of "white flight" that has decimated the Motor City's tax base and led to a downward spiral of hopelessness and crime.*

I wasn't sure I understood all that but I kept reading because it was almost like hearing Mom's voice. She talked about how, back in the 1940s, Detroit had been mostly white, and that black people started moving up from the south to get jobs and escape the harsh Jim Crow laws. I knew about those from Mr. Howard's class about segregation and the Ku Klux Klan, and how being black in some states was worse than being a second-class citizen. It could get you killed. But as I read on, it didn't sound a whole lot better in Detroit where these newcomers were shut out of all sorts of things, from jobs to housing and even supermarkets, and ended up being herded together in neighborhoods where there wasn't much opportunity. It was called redlining, which made me think of what teachers do to some poor kid's paper when they don't think he's up to snuff.

"What's that about?" Sabrina said, startling me so that the papers seized up in my hands.

"Jeez, give a person a heart attack," I complained, but then I told her about what I had read.

"Have you ever been there?" she asked. She sank down to sit beside me, her face rapt.

I told her about the time we had gone to a concert in Detroit, about all the concrete and the overpasses scrawled with graffiti like strange flowers, and the enormous black man who had tipped his fancy hat to me as we'd crossed a street.

"He had on a full-length fur coat," I said, "and when he smiled, I saw a bunch of gold teeth."

I could tell she didn't believe that part, but it was true, and it had made me feel the strangeness of the city in my bones, what with the long Buicks and Cadillacs nosing down the street like it was a river, and the distant cry of sirens, and somewhere nearby, the shunting of rail cars, booming like the beat of a drum.

"Maybe we could call the phone numbers on your list instead," Sabrina said, as if she could see the picture in my mind. She was trying to sound reasonable but I could tell reality was finally dawning on her. Nipping over to Detroit for a look-see was sounding less appealing by the minute.

That's when I told her my idea about the postcards.

"Even better," she said with relief as we boxed everything up again and headed for the stairs. "Only you should use some secret name, you know, that only the two of you would recognize. That way, if she's trying to protect you and your dad's identity from the bad guys, you won't blow her game."

That was really smart, which is what I relied on Sabrina for. I was so excited to get started on my first postcard, I almost chucked her out the door.

"Alright, already, a person can take a hint!" she said, but I could tell she was laughing inside.

"See you tomorrow," I said, then shut the door on Sabrina and the blustery day, on billows of cherry blossoms coming off the trees like dreaming, and hurried upstairs to get to work.

# EIGHT
# *Thoughts*

Maybe writing all those postcards stirred up a lot of feelings, because the next afternoon, I decided I needed a long bike ride. I like to get lost on my rides, even though that's hard to do in a town like Fairview. I'll pedal over hills and duck into alleys, cut through empty lots and mix it all up like I'm wrapping a big ball of thread. If I'm lucky, there will be at least one moment when I'm not sure how to get home. It's best to do on a rainy day when the sky is gray and cozy overhead and the smell of wet earth is in the air. You splash through puddles and get as wet as you can, and by the time you get home, it feels like you've gone twice as far as you really did, especially with your pj's on and a cup of warm tea in your hands.

Today, it was sunny, but beggars can't be choosers. I needed to think.

Thinking is hard to understand. Most people just have thoughts. I'm not saying I'm a genius, but even I can tell the difference between what's real and a thought that's just passing through. This may seem obvious enough, and for a long time, I thought everybody knew it, but when I was six, I made a tremendous discovery. Adults actually *believe* their thoughts. And not just the adults who stand on street corners, conversing with the lamp post. No, even ordinary folks are looking at their thoughts the whole time they're looking at your face, saying whatever it is they're saying.

That must be why they fight so much, because nobody's script matches up, and so everyone stalks around, slapping the page in their head with the back of their hand like they can't believe their ears. When I first discovered this, I wanted to snap my fingers in front of their noses, but now I'm worried about when it will kick in for me, and I'll start looking at *my* thoughts instead of the world around me. I'm hoping the fact that I've noticed will protect me, like a vaccination shot.

What *I* mean by thinking is more like *feeling*, or maybe asking a question that never gets answered. When I really get going, it's amazing what I find out. Today, I started out thinking about Mom, but ended up pondering Leanne and the nature of her soul. Only I didn't have enough information, so most of what I learned was about me.

To top it all off, I didn't get lost once.

When I pulled up in front of our house at 38 Rosemary Street, there was Gloria's orange Nova, parked out at the curb. She could afford to drive anything, but she drives a Nova because she thinks it's sporty. I stood there, straddling my bike for a while as I thought about how I could get up to my room without being seen. Finally, I stepped off, then wheeled my bike slowly up the side of the house to the backyard, where I left it leaning against the oak.

The one pity about old houses is they creak a lot. The hinges creak and the floorboards creak, and by the time I got up the hall to the bottom of the stairs, I figured they must have gone deaf not to hear me, wheezing along. But as it turns out, they were having a "discussion," so that explains it.

"Do you *realize*," Gloria said, dragging out the word like it had four syllables, "that she won't even get into a *car*?"

That was, frankly, none of her business. If I didn't much care for vehicular transportation, that was nobody's business but my own. I parked it on the stairs to hear what else was brewing.

"She's working through things in her own way,

Gloria," Dad said, and I could hear him flirting with third gear.

"Working through, or avoiding?" Gloria said. "That child needs to go to a psychiatrist."

*Now*, I was listening. So was Dad.

"Are you nuts?" he said, losing his cool. "You want to throw that in the mix? Listen, Gloria, she's my daughter, and I will parent her in my own way."

"Then *parent* her, for chrissake," she said, and I knew she was just dying to take a long drag off a cigarette, but Dad won't allow smoking in the house. "What are you doing with all these . . . these . . . *things* anyway?"

Uh oh. That did it.

"That thing is my art," Dad said, hitting the gear shift full throttle. The conversation was now officially over. They exchanged a few more words, but Gloria knew it too. She's known Dad a long time.

Sometimes, I wonder how Mom turned out so well with a mom like Gloria. She's a beautiful woman, but somehow that beauty never gets inside, just sits on top like a bunch of makeup she's slapped on. Dad used to say that a woman isn't really beautiful until she ages and her life shows on her face, which is the kind of theory artists have. He would look at Mom as he said it, like he could already see their whole life written there, the one they'd spent together, making her eyes crinkly and deep and creasing the sides of her face. But I can't quite see it with Gloria. Maybe it has to be the right kind of life. Or, maybe that's not the kind of beauty he was talking about.

After Gloria was gone, I let out a long breath between my teeth. I could hear Dad fumbling around with his paint brushes, trying to get back in the mood.

A psychiatrist?

As if that was going to change anything. I could picture myself lying back on a long couch and telling the shrink everything that was in my head. That part wasn't so bad, but I was pretty sure he, or she, would try to pick me apart and rearrange me, like a giant puzzle. The truth is, for all my faults, I'm happy with the way I am. The very thought gave me a chill, so I decided to tread carefully. Dad had my back, but when Gloria got an idea in her head, she was like a force of nature.

I was feeling softhearted toward Dad because of how he'd stuck up for me, so I went back down the hall, then pretended I was coming in for the first time.

"Hi Dad," I said, and went right over to sit on his knee. He didn't say anything, just put down his brush and slid his arms around my stomach, resting his chin in the crook of my neck. I leaned my head against the side of his and we sat there for the longest time, looking at all those galaxies, big and small, saying nothing together. Mom and I used to talk up a storm, but this is what Dad and I do best, when I can catch him in the right mood. He cinched his arms tighter, as if I might slip away, so I nestled in, just so he'd know I wasn't going anywhere.

After about fifteen minutes, we both knew it was over, at the same, exact time. He kissed me on the cheek and I hopped up, fixing to get my pjs on even though I hadn't gotten wet. Tomorrow was a big day.

We were going to have our very first rehearsal!

# NINE
# A Door in the World

I got to the auditorium early this time.

I was feeling jittery, so I decided to meet my nerves head on. There's something soothing about sitting alone in a big, empty theater with the half-lights up, that musty smell coming off the seats, and the echo of footsteps far away. I took deep breaths and tried to get in character.

"Show time!" Sabrina said as she plopped down beside me.

I jolted in my seat, then gave her a mock glare. "Someone's feeling chipper."

"There's nothing like the prospect of schlepping sets around to give one's life meaning," she said with a smirk. "That and repairing all the broken mop handles Colin and Davis have been jousting with."

I giggled. Being with Sabrina makes me feel bolder. Lately I've been joking around with Colin and Davis too, or at least Colin, because Davis only relates to other people through him.

"Well, I'm just glad you're here." I slid lower in my seat as Harry walked by, followed by Jenny Pippin and the twins. Then I heard Karen's voice booming down the aisle and sank as low as I could while still looking like a normal person. But she walked right on by. Leanne followed a few minutes later with a clipboard in hand, and I almost waved.

"There's your new friend," Sabrina said.

Irony is Sabrina's forte. But she meant what she said in the tube that day, about me branching out, so she's decided to give Leanne a chance. One thing about Sabrina, she's not the jealous type.

"Where should I put my notebook?" I asked, half to change the subject, and half because I was afraid Karen might steal it.

Sabrina narrowed her eyes and scanned the theater for a glimpse of Karen. "Quick, while she's holding Cory in a headlock. Just stash it between the cushions."

I acted fast, then the two of us got up all nonchalant and headed to the front two rows where the cast was assembling.

"Excited?" Miss Gorman gave us all a good going-over. I let my eyes say it all because my mouth wasn't working. "Great. Who's learned their lines for the first scene?"

I snaked my hand up, looking around to see if I was the odd one out. Sure enough, more than a few people would be needing prompts. Miss Gorman nipped that one in the bud with a short lecture about how the real work started when everyone was on the mat, or in this case, stage. But even her lectures felt like pep talks.

"Let's run it!" she said, and sent us up to take our marks.

I'd run the scene a gazillion times in my head, mostly while watching the squirrels, but as I walked up those stairs, I worried that I wouldn't be able to recapture the magic. What if my audition was a fluke? What if I turned out to be boring and stiff, like a cadaver gussied up in a little, green suit?

"Melanie," Miss Gorman said, startling me out of my thoughts. She had come up from behind and was leaning down to speak confidentially. "How would you feel about cutting your hair?"

Was that all? I thought she was about to break the bad news, that it was all a mistake and I was going to understudy for the croc instead.

"Sure!" I said, wanting to show off my professionalism. I look like a pixie anyway because I'm small and skinny and have mousy, flat hair. What was a few inches off the top?

"Excellent, I'll bring you some pictures of what we're going for."

That was that, and we all took our marks in the nursery, even though the furniture was just taped off on the floor. Karen walked right through Wendy's bed and leaned over her knees, running fingers through her hair and then flipping it back as she stood so that all the feathery parts settled down. She does that all the time.

"Ready, Laurelann," she said with a smile.

This was going to take some top-notch imagining. Nobody was where they were supposed to be. Jimmy Flanders, who plays the youngest Darling, Michael, was picking his nose in the corner, which was sort of in character, but David, who played John, was just lounging against a post. Cory Plath was bounding around the stage, licking everyone's knees. The part of Nana is supposed to be played by a dog, so kudos to Cory for method acting, but come on, people, some order please?

I caught sight of Sabrina in the wings, and I couldn't help it. I rolled my eyes.

"Have you got something in your eye, Melanie?" Karen said, like a mother fussing over a cranky infant. "Or is there something you'd like to share with the cast?"

A cold shaft of fear went right through me. Karen was out to make me look like a prima donna in front of Miss Gorman, so I would have to watch out. And she wasn't going to be calling me Smellanie up here, either. She knows her audience.

"No, *there*, I've got it," I said, cupping my eye and leaning forward as if I'd just got a bit of dust out. She had met her match in me.

"Now, kids, remember what we talked about," Miss Gorman was saying. "Pretend the curtain is down and take your positions. You've got to really picture the scene and anticipate what comes next."

There was some milling around, but just when I thought we were ready, the auditorium doors burst open and Colin and Davis came barreling down the aisle.

"The aliens have landed!" Davis cried, running ahead and waving his arms.

"Take-me-to-Mc-Don-alds," Colin said in a robot voice, following behind with jerking footsteps and bent elbows.

"Late," Miss Gorman said, and gave them both a slip when they reached the stage. You've got to hand it to Miss Gorman, she's got backbone.

*Finally*, we were ready.

"I won't go to bed, I won't," Jimmy said, stomping his foot. "Nana, it isn't six o'clock yet. Um, line?"

"Two more minutes . . ." Miss Gorman said.

"Oh, yeah, two more minutes Nana, please? I won't take a bath, I won't!"

I was standing in the wings, waiting for my cue, when I realized Leanne was watching quietly beside me. I wanted to say something, but I had no idea what, so we just kept watching together as Cory started bounding again, turning down the beds with his mouth and then nudging the taps for Michael's bath with his snout. Jeanette took the stage as Mrs. Darling and walked over to the window because she'd just seen a face.

"Who are you?" she said, then, "No one there. And yet, I feel sure I saw a face." Jeanette's good at pretending to be an adult. She's very bland.

Now it was Karen's turn to shine, at least that's what she was telling herself. She and the other children went around playing at dolls, while Harry wandered in as Mr. Darling, his square head a perfect match for the role. Before I knew it, the younger Darlings were all in bed.

This was it.

I could feel the weight of destiny upon me as I pictured the darkened nursery, steeped in mystery, and the wind rising in the trees outside.

"Leanne," Miss Gorman called out. "This is where the spotlight comes in, darting around the chest of drawers. Can you make a note of that?"

Leanna scribbled something on her clipboard. Show biz was full of interruptions, I thought, but it didn't take me long to get back on track.

I imagined the light that was Tinker Bell, flitting about the room.

The windows blew open.

And there I was, crouched on the threshold, whispering, "Tinker Bell, Tink, are you there?"

I don't know what I was worried about. There's a door in the world, right there for anyone to see. I wasn't in the theater at all, but in a place where the shadows were deeper and the smells richer, a place where possibility lurked in every corner and made ordinary things come to life. All of London was spread out behind me, rising rooftop by rooftop to the starry sky. There was a sausage shop across the street and carriages rattling by the park of dark, rustling trees. And I wondered why people didn't come here all the time when the real world was so washed out and bright, what with that door standing open the whole time and a lifetime of mystery beyond.

"Boy, why are you crying?" Karen barked, ruining the mood. Technically, that *was* her line, but she gave me the stink eye when she said it. I pretended she had a pitiable ocular condition that was inoperable. Working with Karen was going to be a trial, but I figured my imagination was a match for her lack of one.

Then, she whispered something distinctly off-script.

"I'm coming for you, Smellanie." It hissed out while the other Darlings were messing about onstage, and for a moment, the magic wavered, like a mirage in the desert, hovering over the blazing road. "You better toughen up, or you're going down."

Why couldn't she leave me alone? Why was she looking at me like I'd stolen her prized possession when she was the one always angling for my notebook? The injustice of it stung, and I could feel my eyes stinging too. Maybe reality was just a barren stretch of sand and sky, after all, with no one looking down on you but that brutal sun, shriveling it all to dust. I was beginning to feel pretty sorry for myself when I thought suddenly of Sabrina, clowning around in the last row. What a kick in the rear end she'd have given me right about now, if only she knew!

So I swiped my eyes on the sly and gave Karen a glare that said *bring it on*, even though that wasn't how I felt.

And off I went, leaping around the stage, sprinkling pixie dust wherever I went. That's what Peter Pan does. And one way or another this was going to be fun.

TEN

# On the Subject of Souls

Saturday rolled around before I knew it.

I wasn't sure if I was dreading or looking forward to going to Leanne's house. Maybe both, but I was mostly dreading it because of all the things that could go wrong. We might have nothing to say to each other, or we might not like what the other person said. Worst of all, she might decide she'd made a mistake, inviting me over, even if Miss Gorman had put her up to it.

"What do you think she wants?" Sabrina had said on Friday afternoon.

"Does she have to want something?" I said, even though I had been secretly wondering myself.

"Then why the big change?" she persisted. "She never used to give you the time of day."

"You're the one who said I should take more risks!" I snapped, but Sabrina just shrugged.

"Just thinking out loud," she said, all mopey, but not for long because she couldn't keep a straight face. Sabrina's good about admitting when she's wrong.

Saturday morning I woke up extra early and tried on all my clothes. This didn't take long, but I went through several rounds, trying to decide which corduroys to wear. For a split second, I wished I had a pair of San Francisco Riding Gear jeans like Karen's. They have a buckle on the back, and the legs are wide all the way down, like an elephant. That might sound kind of goofy, but they're all the rage. Only I know I wouldn't feel like myself, even if we could afford them. You'd think someone with such a good imagination would enjoy feeling like somebody else, but you can't put lipstick on a pig.

Finally, I decided on my maroon cords and my sunset T-shirt with the pretty pastels.

The bike ride to Leanne's house took a while, even without getting lost. I knew, more or less, where she lived, way up in the hills. It's a newer neighborhood, and I could tell I was getting close when the houses all started to look alike, side by side on their tidy lawns, as if they'd sprung up when nobody was looking. I call them doppelganger houses. A doppelganger is somebody's soulless, evil twin. It looks exactly the same as a real person, with the same face and hair, the same way of walking and talking, except that it's hungry all the time, which is what comes of not having a soul. And of course, the eyes are all wrong, because you can't hide something like that.

I pulled up in front of 3785 Mulberry Lane. It was a nice street name, written neatly on the scrap of paper Leanne gave me, so I was hoping for the best. The house was white with columns around the porch and windows like big, sightless eyes, just like the J. C. Penney building downtown, reflecting the sky. Only, there you could imagine ghosts floating from floor to floor, remembering the good old days when the lunch counter was full and the elevators went up and down, jam-packed with people, whereas this house couldn't even remember its own name.

I parked my bike as neatly as I could around the side, then walked up the flight of steps.

"Is Leanne home?" I said when the door opened.

The woman was wiping her hands on a towel, squinting as if she couldn't quite make me out from so far away. Then, she looked over her shoulder and called, "Leanne!" She stepped aside for me to enter. Leanne came down the stairway that was right inside the front door, her feet silent on the thick, white carpet.

"Hi," I said and cringed. I sounded like a poor mouse somebody was strangling. Leanne's mom had already turned around and headed back towards the kitchen or the den or wherever it was she'd been sitting when I rang, probably reading a magazine. She had heels on, but you couldn't hear the click clack because of the wall-to-wall carpet.

I could feel that house start sucking on my soul the moment I walked in, as if it hadn't had a meal in ages.

"Come on up to my room," Leanne said and turned around, waving for me to follow. I looked down at my shoes, then took them off, setting them beside the door. I hadn't thought to wear my best socks, and they looked kind of threadbare, but at least my toes weren't sticking out.

Leanne's room was exactly what I had expected.

There was the lavender, canopied bed, its bedspread, all sprinkled with purple flowers. The windows had frilly curtains beneath a valance, and the desk was white and glossy. I was afraid to sit on anything, just in case I had mud on my pants from riding my bike. But Leanne was already sitting cross-legged in the middle of the bed with her binder open before her, so I settled there too, leaning over to see.

"Laurelann gave me an extra few days to finish my creative writing assignment," she explained, "because I was having trouble with it."

"That was nice of her," I said, feeling a little ray of sunshine at the thought of Miss Gorman.

"She's my favorite teacher," Leanne said, leafing through her binder. A second little ray of sunshine joined the first.

"Me too." I was glad we had something in common.

Leanne looked up at me with her dark, blue eyes. "I just don't know how to get started."

The thing about Leanne is that she's really pretty. I would have told her she looks just like Cheryl Ladd who plays Kris on *Charlie's Angels*, but Kris is a disaster, and I wouldn't want to insult her. Leanne has the same long blond hair and straight nose, and on the rare occasion that she smiles, she looks like a toothpaste model, with the light glinting off her teeth in gaudy sparkles.

"Well," I said, "you start with an idea. What have you thought about?"

Leanne sighed, drumming her eraser on the open page. "That's just it. All my ideas are really boring."

I personally don't think there's any such thing as a boring idea. Watching an ant crawl up the wall can be interesting if you look at it the right way.

"Give me an example," I said, determined to be useful.

Leanne looked at me exactly the way her mom had, like she had glimpsed me from a long way off and was trying to decide if she knew me.

"Okay," she said, then started in about a girl who lived in a castle all alone, way up in the sky. It sounded a lot like some other stories I had heard, but it was a good place to start, and I told her so.

"You just have to find the soul of the story," I said and immediately turned red because I hadn't meant to say so much. Talking about souls isn't something you do, even in experimental schools. But she seemed to take it in stride, so I plunged on. "What I mean is that you ask the story to tell you what it is. You can't order it around, because you don't know what it is yet, do you? So you have to listen."

I was babbling like the village idiot, but she nodded in understanding. We talked some more about writing, about metaphors and similes, which we had studied in class. I tried to make her understand that they weren't just words with definitions that you filled in on a test. They were windows into other worlds.

"It's a way that something can be two things at once," I explained. "Like if I said an orange looked like a sun, all of a sudden, it isn't the same orange." It was a rotten simile, but she took my point.

"I feel like everyone will know I don't know how to do this," Leanne said, and I didn't know what to say about that.

By the end of the hour, she had a decent story about a girl who spent so much time up in her sky-castle that she became a cloud. That part Leanne got all on her own, and it was really good.

"I can't believe I wrote this," she said. She was just staring at the page with a funny kind of glow all over her face. "Are you hungry?"

"You bet," I said, even though I wasn't. I figured her mom was still lurking downstairs, using the Cuisinart or maybe pasting pictures from catalogs into her lifestyle journal. I wasn't sure what moms like her did. Besides, her dad might be around too, and he seemed just as scary. It was probably my imagination getting the better of me, but with doppelganger houses, you never know.

Sure enough, they were both in the kitchen. We had to pussyfoot around while we made ourselves peanut butter and jelly sandwiches. They didn't say anything to each other or to us, just kept right on with what they were up to. I nailed it about the catalog because that's exactly what Leanne's mother was leafing through, though she wasn't cutting anything out. Leanne's dad was on the phone, sitting in the breakfast nook with the cord pulled tight around the corner as he nodded his head, listening and kicking his crossed leg, up and down.

It was a relief to go sit in the dining room.

"It's some girl from that school," I heard Leanne's mother say through the door, talking to Leanne's dad after he'd gotten off the phone. She didn't sound impressed, but I couldn't tell if it was me or the school that had let her down.

Leanne looked at me sidelong like she'd heard it too. I had wondered why Leanne was at Buckminster when she didn't seem to belong there. Now, it occurred to me that maybe she chose it herself.

"Good sandwich," I said.

After that, we played some board games up on her bed, Life and then Battleship. It was getting on in the afternoon, and I didn't want to overstay my welcome.

"Well, I hope that helped," I said as I stood again on her doorstep with my shoes back on. Leanne had her hand on the door, and she had fixed me again with that faraway look, only this time it reminded me of someone stuck in the bottom of a well, looking upward toward the light. I'd read about a kid who fell in a well one time, and they didn't find him for days, so he just had to sit there in the muddy water, watching that circle of sky go from light to dark to light again. "See you," I said, and turned to go.

I was halfway down the steps when she said my name.

"Thanks a lot," she said. "You're really nice." Then she nipped inside and closed the door behind her.

I stood there, just staring at the house, trying to figure out how I felt. But after a while, those blank windows spooked me, so I ducked around the side of the house for my bike, then headed for home.

# ELEVEN
## *The Invitation*

I don't know what I was expecting.

Monday, at school, I went from class to class as usual, sitting at my desk with Sabrina while Leanne sat next to Karen and Kim, working at her binder like there was something extra interesting written there.

"Hi Leanne," I said during math and gave her a little wave. We had just finished up our multiplication drill, and Mr. Funkel was fixing to break out the word problems.

She waved back and smiled, and that was enough to make Karen frown and look back and forth between us, as if she'd unearthed a dastardly plot. Leanne's pale cheeks turned red. Then, Mr. Funkel came down the aisle with the word problem, one of those process-of-elimination scenarios, you know, where Johnny is sitting next to Jackie and Jenny, but not Geraldine, and you have to figure out what they all had for lunch. I usually love these problems, and I made my table to X off the possibilities, but it just didn't feel the same.

"I thought you said it went well," Sabrina whispered, leaning over.

"I helped her out, so what," I said, hoping the subject was closed.

The rest of the day was pretty much the same, except for guitar when Leanne tossed me a few more smiles. I smiled back, but I didn't want to be one of those people who will pounce on any old scrap people throw their way.

I was walking away from school when I realized I wasn't alone.

"Hey Smellanie, wait up," I heard, and my blood froze, like when you're watching an old black-and-white movie and a skeletal hand comes reaching around the corner.

Slowly, I turned.

There was Karen, all on her own, swinging her arms la-de-dah as she strolled up for a chat.

"I was thinking we should get to know each other a little better," she said, a smile pasted on her mulish face. "Maybe I've been a little hard on you, huh?"

There was syrup in her voice, as if she were a therapist on daytime TV. I knew it was a load of hooey, but there were too many things running through my head to pick just one, and my heart was still thudding in my ears.

"Oh, come on," Karen said, kind of cozy and whiny, "you're not going to hold a grudge, are you? What can I do to make it up to you?"

"You could stop calling me Smellanie."

The words were out before I knew it, and I felt this wave of energy, like lightning shooting out of my ears. I don't think Karen was expecting it either because, for a second, she frowned, then got the smile back in place with a few tugs.

"You shouldn't feel bad about that," she said. "I give all my friends nicknames."

That one was so dumb I just let it stand.

There we were in the middle of the sidewalk with kids milling around us, passing us by, and a few of them wondering what was up. Karen was eyeing me like one of the squirrels from my tree, turning an acorn around in her paws and looking for a way in—if squirrels were capable of unspeakable evil, that is, which they aren't.

"All right, I'll tell you the truth," she said. "Leanne asked me to be nice to you. Don't you think we should both try, for her sake?"

Maybe I wanted this to be true. I could hear Sabrina in my head, telling me not to be a dope, but I let Karen talk anyway.

"A few of us are going to the skating rink later today," she said. "Why don't you come?"

It occurred to me that maybe Karen was smiling like a zombie that had undergone facial reconstruction because she felt as awkward as I did. Besides, she wasn't used to smiling. Maybe it hurt.

"I'll see," I said and gave a shrug. "I'll see if I can."

"Don't forget," Karen said, strolling off as if I'd already said yes. "Five sharp."

All the way home, I went up and down and round and round in my head, until I thought I might throw up. One minute I was thinking Leanne must have put Karen up to it and the next I was back to smelling a rat. The worst thing was I couldn't know which was true without going to the skating rink. If I didn't go, Leanne might think I didn't want to be friends, and all of a sudden I knew that I wanted to be friends with Leanne, more than anything in the world.

Well, almost anything else.

That started me thinking about Mom again and wishing I could ask her for advice. Missing your mom is like realizing, all of a sudden, that you only have one lung. It's bad. So I was glad when Sabrina came up alongside me, just as I turned onto Rosemary Street.

"Oh, boy," she said, taking one look at my face. "Okay, out with it."

"I received an . . . invitation," I said, then told her the scoop. She narrowed her eyes and started shaking her head, back and forth, back and forth, so that her dark hair swished around her shoulders. I could tell she was already thinking how dopey I was.

"You laughed in her face, I hope," she said, and I must have shuffled my feet a bit, because she rolled her head back to gape at the sky, then brought her gaze down with an *I can't believe you* kind of stare.

"*Melanie!*"

"I did ask her to stop calling me Smellanie," I said, feeling bristly.

"And did she say she would?"

I couldn't answer that honestly, so I said nothing. Sabrina must have relented, because she threw an arm around my shoulder and led me up the path to the house.

"I can see you've made your mind up, even if you can't," she said, chuckling like there was no accounting for the behavior of certain primitive lifeforms. But I was willing to be condescended to, because after all, fair is fair. If it looks like a dope and talks like a dope, it must be a dope.

But I had to try.

"Can you help me get ready?" I asked, and then we went inside.

***

I didn't ask Dad for permission. He'd started on a new quadrant of his painting, so he'd be miles away by now, and I knew he'd say yes, without quite hearing what I'd said. He didn't used to be like that when Mom was around, back in the good old days, and I felt for him, but sometimes my sorry feelings got knotted up with being mad and sad until all I wanted to do was chuck the whole mess out the window and read a book.

I cinched the back door shut and grabbed my bike, patting the change purse in my pocket. I'm a big saver, so I had more than enough cash. Sabrina had offered to come, but I knew I had to do this alone, and besides, I'm the one Karen invited. My heart was thumping in time as I pedaled down the street, turning onto Main and then heading out in the direction of the mall. There's a bike path by the river that takes you right there, so I didn't have to deal with many cars, and before I was even ready, there I was, pulling up to Race-n-Skate, its parking lot half-full and its billboard missing a few letters so that the message never quite makes sense.

Inside, the lobby was cool and dark. I took off my shoes and went over to the shelves, selecting skates in my size and tucking them under my arm as I crossed to the counter to pay. The lady behind the register eyed me up and down, like she couldn't get my number, which seemed strange, but I smiled extra nice to help her out. Maybe she was just one of those cranky types.

"You one of the party?" she asked, suspiciously.

I felt a jolt and wondered if Karen had planned more than I'd bargained for. Had she invited half the class? I fought the wave of panic that followed. The smell of rat was all around me now, but what else could I do?

"I think so," I said, and the lady shrugged, took my five-dollar bill, and handed me the change. Not looking at my face, she yanked her head toward the entrance to the rink.

"They're already in there," she said.

I could hear the ruckus even before I crossed the threshold into the rink, which was brighter than the lobby and hurt my eyes. I blinked a few times and walked forward, still holding the skates under my arm. It took me a minute to understand the forms I saw buzzing around, some arm in arm, others kind of creaky like they'd be going down any minute. That's when the schmaltzy music registered in my ears, and I looked up into the stands to see Karen and Kim, sitting in the front row with their feet up on the rail, laughing like it was going out of style.

Time slowed down for what seemed like an eternity but was probably only two seconds. It was open and airy in there, inside my big moment, so I had lots of time to think. Part of me wanted to turn and run right out of the rink because I could see that the party was some kind of geriatric reunion, and all the skaters were about 102. My eyes stung, but mostly I was mad at myself for being such a dope, and mad at Leanne too, even though I didn't know if she'd had anything to do with it. Who cared what Karen thought, but my skin was crawling at the idea that maybe Leanne knew I was a dope too, and after all, who likes someone who can't respect herself?

I just stood there getting madder and madder as the skaters creaked by, bent over in case they fell, while Karen and Kim laughed and pointed and the whole scene spun in my mind like a merry-go-round, out of control.

"Melanie?"

I looked up. I was standing at the bottom of the short staircase that gives onto the rink, and there was my old friend, Mr. Baum, with his rheumy eyes and grand, wrinkly smile, pulling over with one swoop of his leg.

"Oh! Mr. Baum. Hi," I said and flashed on that time I had helped him open up his shoe repair store one Saturday morning when I was tired of watching the squirrels.

"What a pleasure to see you, young lady," he said, very civilized, like he always is. "Would you like to take a turn?" He gestured about the rink with one liver-spotted hand, gnarly from decades of fixing shoes, but with a graceful flick of his wrist, because Mr. Baum had class.

All of a sudden, I plopped down on the stair and jammed on my skates, lacing them tight. Why should I give Karen and Kim the satisfaction of seeing me bolt off, all boohoo and woe-is-me? They'd already had their fun. It was time I had mine.

I knew Sabrina would be proud.

Off we went, sailing out into the sea of old ladies and men. It was cozy and sweet because, as you've probably guessed, I like old things. They were throwing me smiles as Mr. Baum and I skated by, side by side. Then I zipped off and meandered through the crowd, arms clutched behind the small of my back, just like an ice skater from the days of yore when these folks were kids too.

When I looked up at the stands, Karen and Kim weren't laughing.

When I looked up a second time, they were gone.

## TWELVE
# *Forgotten Places*

The next day, Leanne kept trying to catch my eye. I could feel her glancing over during math, and I could feel how grumpy Karen was too, all without looking up, because I'd never been so interested in long division. Sometimes, when I'm confused, I just put myself in a little box and set it to the side.

It was a B day, so after math I headed to Mr. Howard's room. Our electives are divided into A and B days so we can cram more activities into our day-to-day lives. Buckminster Fuller was what some people call a renaissance man, which means he wanted to do everything under the sun, and I'm like that too. I wish I had an extra few lives lying around somewhere so I could be an actress and an explorer and a diplomat, and maybe run for president, all while I'm washing my hair and brushing my teeth.

Today's elective was called Radio Drama: Adventures in the Mind's Eye. It seemed like the whole class was in it, because who wouldn't want to sign up for a class called that? Just people with no imagination, I suppose, like Karen and Kim, who were taking basket weaving instead.

People were still filing in when Leanne sat down at the desk beside me.

*"Ahem,"* Sabrina said from my other side, but I just ignored her. I couldn't bring myself to open the box I'd put myself in, so I just got out a sheet of paper and doodled.

"Okay class, here we go," Mr. Howard said when everyone was settled. Down went the lights and up came the recording, scratchy, like the air was on fire. It was exciting as the first few bars of music played, and then a voice, deep and mysterious, said, "*The shadow knooooows*."

I could tell we were in for a real creep-fest, and I almost forgot about Leanne sitting there beside me.

*The Shadow* is my favorite radio drama. It's about this detective who can become invisible, a convenient skill when you're out to solve crimes. This episode featured a spooky person who lived in a mirror, and I could just see that greenish face, rising out of the dark classroom like it was the mirror itself, along with blood-curdling laughter. It was almost *too* spooky. I was glad when the lights came up.

That's when I remembered Leanne sitting there, and I couldn't gather up my books fast enough.

I don't know what I was afraid of. It wasn't like I had done anything wrong. Leanne was the one who maybe was or maybe wasn't in on Karen's plot to make me look like a fool. I could have just asked her, and I knew Sabrina was shaking her head behind me as we filed out of class, but the whole thing was too hot to touch.

I hurried through the whole day just like that, and at long last, the final bell rang.

"Come on, let's go do something," Sabrina said, rushing up beside me as I was walking away. The regular school kids get out ten minutes after we do, and I like to get away before then because it's such a zoo.

"Okay, sure," I said and gave her a grateful smile. There are a lot of things I like about school, but on days like this, I can feel things lighten up with every step I take away from that low slung, brick building, as if I were an astronaut breaking free from its gravitational pull.

It was good to be going home.

"What do you want to do?" Sabrina asked as we turned onto Rosemary Street.

I knew just the thing. It was something I hadn't done in ages, because it was a little babyish, but I didn't think Sabrina would mind.

"Let's play jewel factory," I said and led her right past my house to the old alley that cuts between Rosemary and Lavender streets.

Remember how I was talking about forgotten places, and how the side yard qualifies as one even though we use it all the time? The alley is another one. Forgotten places are chock full of magic, which accumulates in direct proportion to neglect. This is just one of the many principles scientists have yet to discover because, although scientists are very good at dicing up the physical world, they don't know what to do with the insides of things.

The alley has two bumpy ruts of dried mud, surrounded by all sorts of green things that can't wait to take over again. The air smells like lilacs, which has to be the dreamiest smell known to mankind. I guided Sabrina to a place beside the old fence where people have dumped broken glass for years and years, as if, by means of some secret agreement, they all understood it was meant to be.

"This is the jewel factory," I said, glad to see it was just as I'd left it. I sat down cross-legged on a tuft of grass and patted the ground beside me. "These are the diamonds and rubies, and these are the emeralds and amber," I explained, separating out the piles by color and starting to mine from the big mishmash that had yet to be excavated. Already, I could feel the magic taking over, even though there's not much going on in the game, and I don't know why it feels so good. It must be another door in the world, because the minute I start imagining, everything changes, not just the piles of glass but the trees and the sky and all of the houses, as if they all live in another dimension, one that's both brighter and deeper than the day-to-day world.

"Um, hi Melanie. Um . . . can we talk?"

When I looked up, I couldn't believe my eyes. There was Leanne, straddling her bike and looking down at our game. I couldn't even get it together to say anything, which she must have taken personally, because her cheeks flared bright red. They do that a lot.

"I didn't even know about it until Kim told me this morning," she blurted, clutching the hand grips of her bike until her knuckles turned white. "Oh, Melanie, I'm so sorry. I don't know why Karen's so mean to you. I think she's just jealous of you."

This was way, way too much information to process. I figured my brain center would be down for good.

Leanne must have thought I wasn't going to forgive her, because she started to turn the front wheel of her bike to go.

"Anyway, I just wanted you to know," she said. She was almost off and out of my life forever when Sabrina nudged me, hard, then gave me bug-eyes while yanking her head.

"That's okay," I managed, croaky, like I hadn't talked in a year. "I figured you didn't know anything about it." A little white lie wouldn't hurt anyone.

Her face turned back, and her blue eyes were wide. I could tell she was trying to say something else, but couldn't figure out what, and all of a sudden, I just wanted to help her out.

Leanne's really different up close.

"Do you— do you want to play for a while?" I said, hardly realizing that the words were out until . . . there they were, dangling in the air between us.

Her blue eyes got even wider.

"Sure," she said, less carefully. "Sure, I'd love to."

Sabrina started pointing at the piles of glass. "We were just playing this game. It's called— "

"Did you ride your bike all the way from your house?" I cut in. I sat there, frozen, like I'd been caught dancing in a room by myself.

"Yeah, I'm pretty fast," she said, which is not what I would have predicted. "I remembered you lived on Rosemary, and I, um, just thought I might get lucky." She swung her leg off her bike, then propped it against the derelict fence post of Mr. Duncan's back yard. "So, what are you doing?"

I felt my face drain.

"As I was *saying*," Sabrina said, with a pointed look in my direction, "we were playing this amazing game called—"

"Actually, just cleaning up." I swept some of the glass bits together with my hands. It would have been a dumb excuse except for all the anti-litter campaigns that were going on these days. "Pretty much done here. What do *you* want to do?"

I could just *feel* Sabrina pressing her lips together beside me. "I'd better be going then," she said, and I suddenly felt really bad, the way I felt that time I got embarrassed about Dad chaperoning a sock hop back in Grayson. He was wearing his arty hat, which is a beat-up fedora, and he didn't look like the other dads in their cardigans and loafers, but the worst thing was how I felt like I'd committed some awful crime just feeling that way, some crime against myself.

I opened my mouth to call out after Sabrina, but with Leanne standing there, it was all I could do to get with the program.

"Can we go to your house?" she said, after Sabrina was out of sight.

"Oh, uh, sure, yeah," I mumbled, as my stomach lurched again. This, frankly, seemed like a worse idea than the jewel factory game, but what could I say?

We walked back up the alley, side by side, Leanne wheeling her bike along. I showed her where to lean it up against the big oak, and then we went in through the back door. The whole time, I was seeing my house through her eyes—the chipped paint and overgrown wisteria, and the homey, lived-in look of the kitchen which would have fit right in fifty years ago but looked a little shabby, now that I had her eyes on.

At least she wouldn't have to remove her shoes.

Mostly, I wasn't keen for her to meet Dad, and it was just like the sock hop all over again, with me feeling guilty and sad. But all the same, I tried to creep past the living room. We'd almost made it to the foot of the stairs when Dad called out.

"Hey, Moo Moo, that you?"

I sighed and turned. There was nothing else for it.

"Hi, Dad," I said, rounding the corner with Leanne in tow.

"Who's this?" Dad said brightly, taking in the two of us. He was standing up with the big brush in hand, and I could see he'd been going at it.

"Wow!" Leanne said, and I gave a start because it came out of nowhere. "Did you make this?"

I had expected Leanne to be shy, meeting my dad, but maybe the shock of seeing a universe all over our wall had snapped her out of it. She was already running her hand over the ridges and valleys, because Dad's paintings are in three dimensions.

"Oh, sorry," she said, and drew her hand back when she realized what she was doing.

Dad laughed. "No, go right on ahead. That's what you're supposed to do. Just steer clear of the wet parts."

After that, the conversation floated right by like a dream, like some ghost writer in the sky had come down to earth just to give me a break. We were all laughing and talking about art and life. Dad was in one of his rare moods. When he uses the big brush, he comes out of his shell.

By the time we got upstairs to my room, I was so happy I could hardly breathe.

"Do you want to play a board game?" I said, thinking about all the ones she had at her house. We only have a few, Scrabble and Yahtzee, and lots of decks that are missing one or two playing cards.

"I don't know," Leanne said, walking around my room with her fingers trailing over the desk and the bookcase, like she couldn't stop touching things after feeling Dad's painting. My room is under the rafters and has all kinds of crazy angles in the ceiling and walls. She seemed to like what she saw, because she stopped in front of my window and looked out at the oak tree with a little smile on her lips, just like that picture of the Mona Lisa. "What was that game you were playing in the alley?" she said, and I could see there was more to Leanne than met the eye.

Like I said, some moments are larger on the inside. I stood there, poised on the edge of things, because the next step was a biggie. I might fall down and down forever, which is how I'd feel if Leanne made fun of me, but I might just float up to the sky where Leanne lived in her cloud house. A few weeks ago, I might have stood there all day, but I guess I'd gotten used to taking steps, even if I didn't know where they led.

"It's this game I play," I said, "called jewel factory," and I told her all about it as we headed downstairs and back out the door.

## THIRTEEN
# *Searching for Clues*

I figured my afternoon with Leanne was a one-off, because for the rest of the week, life went on as usual with Leanne trailing Karen and Kim like some kind of ghost. I could see her trying to send me messages with her eyes and smile, blinking on and off like she was using some kooky Morse code. I decided we were destined to move in different circles, if you could call me and Sabrina a circle. Technically, two points just make a line.

Only, this week, Sabrina was nowhere to be seen.

She'd been cutting school all week, which made me feel sad and confused, thinking it was on account of what had happened with Leanne in the alley. Sabrina's a "take me as I am" kind of person, so she wouldn't understand about me trying to hide my true self. I was trying to be more like her in that way, but I guess it takes time. Then again, Sabrina is an enigma too, so maybe she was ditching school because she was sick with the flu or else helping her pop unload explosives on the night shift.

Not that I believed that stuff.

Like I said, she's a puzzle. When I try to get us talking about *her*, somehow the conversation always turns back round to me. It's like she walks around holding up a big mirror, which is a good way to hide out. Between that and all the stories, I didn't know what to think. Was she really a "take me as I am" kind of person, or was it more like "take me as I want to be"?

I happened to see her walking up Lavender Street early the next Saturday morning, and decided it was high time to figure her out.

Where did she even live? Who were her parents *really*? Maybe she didn't even *have* parents. That seemed right, her being an orphan, like she'd been born one day exactly how she is now and had never gone through the ignominy of sucking her thumb or wetting her pants. I couldn't imagine Sabrina ever sleeping with the light on.

Was she homeless?

I trailed her about a block behind, which felt creepy. Who spies on their best friend? I told myself I was doing it for her sake because, deep down, I sensed she was in trouble. But I have to admit, I was curious too. You can't go around being a secret without having people want to crack the code.

Maybe her family was totally ordinary and she was embarrassed about it.

We'd gone through a few turns and were headed for the dump, which made my arm hairs stand up on end. She couldn't live at the dump, could she? After all, she always looked so put together, just like she'd stepped off a movie set. I kept ducking behind trees as we went because I knew that even if Sabrina was just pretending to be a Charlie's Angel, she was good at it and might already be onto me.

Soon, I saw all the rusted out cars and radiators and old refrigerators moldering in a pile, just over the chain-link fence. There was a mean dog in there too, chewing on a hank of bone that I hoped wasn't someone's femur.

Just at the last moment, she turned left.

Could she be messing with me? The dog was barking like crazy as I caught up to the spot where she'd turned. He was mauling the fence like it was a good day to die. I hustled on past feeling a little sorry because I'm a real animal lover, and I wondered what had happened to make him so mean. Sometimes I wonder if dogs have souls too, and get born with a rotten spot inside, or whether it's just life that roughs them up.

That's when I lost her.

Maybe it was thinking about that dog's rough life that did it, but suddenly I felt so sad. I gazed up Deacon's Butte, which looks out over the whole of Fairview. I thought I saw someone winding through the scraggly maples, flitting up one of the trails, like when a movie projector is turned down slow and the images flick past. A wind blew through, rustling the apple blossoms that were growing wild by the dump, which should have made me happy, but I just wanted to go home.

When I got there, I had a big surprise.

I checked the mailbox, just like I did every morning, and there it was—a postcard from Mom! My hands were shaking as I pulled it out of the pile and slipped it into the back pocket of my cords so I could read it later, in private.

"Hi Dad!" I said, all chipper, when I went in for breakfast. He already had some oatmeal on, so I scarfed that down, then rinsed both our bowls and gave him a salute.

"Where are you off to?" he asked, and really looked at me for a moment. I could tell he'd been daydreaming about his painting all through breakfast and was trying to show some last-minute interest.

But I didn't need that today.

"Just up to my room for a spell," I said, brightly, so he'd know he didn't need to check in on me. I couldn't tell Dad about the postcard, not yet. There had to be some really good reason for Mom to go off like that and leave us all heartbroken. In fact, I could hardly think of a good enough reason. That thought gave me a sad, squirrelly feeling in my stomach, so I put it aside. Suffice it to say, I wasn't about to break her trust.

Upstairs, I did a rolling jump onto my back in the middle of my bed. Outside, I could see the squirrels wrapping up their morning business as I leaned on one hip to snake the postcard out of my pocket, then held it against my heart for a minute, where I could feel the beat.

Slowly, I brought it up for a look.

It was addressed to Nate Prep, which is how I had signed all my postcards to her. That's an anagram of Peter Pan and goofy enough to tip her off that it was a fake name. Mom's a huge sucker for puzzles, so I figured she'd make the connection and know it was from me.

*Dear Nate,* the message began, *the pirates are watching, and the lost boys are in danger. Send smoke signals when you can. Missing you is an arrow in my heart.*

It was signed Lily Tiger. My heart was thumping so hard by the time I'd finished, I was worried I might suffer a cardiac event, so I hoisted myself up to sit and watched the squirrels for a while, slouched over in the middle of my bed with my chin on my knees. That settled me down so I could think clearly.

Could it be that I was right?

That was one possible scenario. If she were really undercover, then the pirates she was talking about would be the Errol Flynns, that Detroit gang that was in the news so much. The lost boys were probably kids the gang was trying to recruit, and the arrow in the heart was her way of telling me she'd be home in a New York minute if there were any other way.

Then again, maybe she was just humoring me.

Isn't that what a good mom would do? Wouldn't she tell her little girl what she wanted to hear? I kept thinking about that night she slammed out of the house and drove off, her voice all shrill because Dad was giving her the silent treatment. Were they arguing about *this*, about Mom wanting to take some risks and make her mark in the news business? Or was it something else?

At least I had an address.

I hopped up to write another postcard and argue my case. She already knew how smart I was, but she probably had doubts about my ability to deal with the real world, so I talked up my new credentials, how I was talking to other kids in class, not to mention starring in the school play. I was pretty tough, these days, and could probably fend for myself by her side. This wasn't strictly true, but I had already changed so much, just since meeting Sabrina, who knew what I could do? I wrote it all in code, just like her, so it was all about Hook and Smee and pixie dust and that kind of stuff. But she'd know what it meant.

It had been quite a morning, and I felt better than I had when I was roaming the neighborhood, searching for Sabrina. I'd even stopped thinking about Leanne and wondering if we were ever going to get around the "Karen problem." There's a saying, *sometimes things go from bad to worse*, but I've found the reverse can be true. And sure enough, when I went downstairs, I had another big surprise waiting for me on the porch.

"Roxie!" I cried and ran right into her arms.

## FOURTEEN
# *Life on the Farm*

Roxie plopped back down in the bright blue rocking chair and started rolling yarn into balls out of her big rattan basket.

"Go get me some coffee," she said with that wry, sideways smile of hers.

"Cream and sugar!" I said, because that's how she takes it. I hustled inside, and soon enough I was back with two steaming mugs. If I were a coffee drinker, I'd take it like Roxie does, which at least makes it taste like ice cream, but I prefer peppermint tea.

Roxie set the yarn in her lap to take the mug, then raised it in a little toast.

"*À santé*," she said, which is fancy for "to your health." Roxie might be a farmer, but she also has a PhD in medieval literature. She teaches part time at the same university where Roland works, but I don't think a person makes much money in that line, and what else can she do except maybe impersonate Maid Marian at some Renaissance fair? So she sells sheep's milk and wool crafts at her Sunday farm stand and gets by just fine.

"What are you doing here?" I asked, when I'd settled into the old, wicker chair. It gave a little wheeze as I nestled in.

Her smile evened out on the other side into a big grin. "The farm, remember? I promised to take you out."

Horse people are surprisingly expert at the care of two-legged creatures, and Roxie always knew how to give me a boost. Maybe some of us are more like horses, bolting at loud noises or loving the feel of the wind on our faces and a scratch on the neck. If I were a horse, I'd probably end up one of those lumpy little Shetlands that are always poking around the barn.

We didn't get going right away. I picked up a skein, and we both sat there, rolling yarn and sipping at our mugs, smelling the blossomy air and just enjoying being quiet together.

Here's a saying everyone knows: *three's a charm*. And sure enough, my third big surprise of the day was just now rounding the bend.

"Who's your friend?" Roxie said.

I looked up to see Leanne standing there, straddling her bike in the middle of our front walk. She looked wary, like maybe she'd been planning on doing a drive-by and getting away before anyone noticed. At least that's what I would have done.

"Hi, Leanne!" I said, extra cheerful so she'd feel welcome, even though inside I felt like I'd stuck my finger in a light socket.

"Hi," she said. The careful voice was back as she eyed Roxie in her muddy boots and canvas coat. "I'm sorry, I didn't know you'd be busy."

"Don't be sorry." Roxie tossed her a mess of yarn, which Leanne fumbled, nearly toppling her bike. "You're just in time to chip in," she said with a wink.

Leanne swung her leg off, then leaned her bike up against the porch. She sat on the bottom stair, untangling the yarn before starting to roll, looking at our hands like she was worried about doing it wrong.

"I'm glad you came by," I said. "We're going to Roxie's farm in a while. You want to come?"

All of a sudden, I was tired of pussyfooting around, and that's when I knew something had changed inside me, without me even knowing it. What did I have to lose? I knew Roxie wouldn't mind, and sure enough she gave a nod with a firm-lipped smile, like she'd thought of it herself.

"Really?" Leanne said, and I could see she was torn. "But I'd have to ask my parents."

"You could call them," I suggested.

It took some wrangling, but after about five minutes, Leanne got the thumbs up. I don't think her parents liked the idea of her gallivanting off with some girl from an experimental school, but they had plans of their own, and busy parents are easy to control.

"They said fine," Leanne said when she hung up, even though I knew they'd said a lot more than that.

We were just walking to the pickup truck when it dawned on me that we'd be *driving* to Roxie's farm. I'd been too excited to think about that, but now, my stomach got tight and my heart skipped a beat or two. Driving didn't use to bother me, but some things are hard to get out of your head, once you think about them, like noticing how weird your tongue feels in your mouth. Driving was like that for me. After all, zipping around in a glorified tin can just doesn't seem natural. But I wasn't about to let that stop me from enjoying what was shaping up to be one of the best days I'd had in a long time. So I took a few deep breaths and piled into the middle of the big front seat.

Roxie's farm is about thirty miles outside of Fairview to the south. We wound up and down green, pastured hills, past all the dots of white sheep and the tumbledown barns. At first, I squinted my eyes, thinking if I couldn't see what was going on, I'd feel better. But then Roxie rolled down the window and turned up the radio, and before I knew it, we were singing *Country Roads* at the top of our voices, right at the same time we were driving on one. What a coincidence.

"Are we almost there?" Leanne said, as we slowed down to take the turn onto Roxie's long, twisty driveway.

Roxie raises sheep and horses, baling hay on the side for extra cash. Her house is so old, I think the ghosts must have lost half their teeth, and that's why the rooms feel whispery, small and musty but full of light, since Roxie doesn't believe in curtains. I get the cozy feeling of olden times every time I walk in, like any minute Ma and Pa Ingalls might come busting through, telling everybody it's time to move out west.

I think Leanne liked it as much as I do.

"What do you think it *is* about horses," I asked as we stood by the white fence, our arms flat on the top rail while we watched Roxie work the horses, round and round.

That wasn't much information to go on, but Leanne knew what I meant.

"That's a good question." She rested her chin on the back of her hand. "I have about a million books at home on raising and feeding them, and all about the different breeds, even though I know I'm never going to get one."

That surprised me. She was even more into horses than I was.

"Reading a book about them is the next best thing," I said, and it actually is, because all the magic comes through.

But Leanne and I didn't need the next best thing that day.

"Alright, girls, I'm ready for you," Roxie said, and we climbed over the fence. She showed us how she'd suited up the horses in their tackle, with the bit in the mouth and the saddle cinched underneath. "Don't be scared, I'm right here," she said and held Daisy by the bit while Leanne put one foot into the stirrup and tried to sling her leg over. It might have been fear on her face or maybe excitement, but her cheeks were flushed, which made her look even prettier than usual.

Soon, we were both up, trotting around the corral like we were born to it. I'd been up on Maribelle a few times before, but I could tell it was Leanne's first ride.

"Hey, you're good at this!" Roxie said as Daisy picked up speed. Leanne just stayed with her, moving up and down like she and Daisy had already worked things out. I felt a flash of pride for her, almost as if I'd done it myself.

"That was *amazing*," she said in a hushed voice when we dismounted.

"You can come back any time," Roxie said. Next to Mom, she's the most generous person in the world.

Leanne and I took a long walk down by the creek, then out to the sheep fields. I showed her the big barn where it feels like angels would sing if they weren't stuck up in heaven. We didn't say much in there, which made me feel even more like we understood each other. Being together without talking is the test of a friendship, and Leanne seemed to know that the big barn was a place for listening.

We were sitting by the creek when she asked me the question I'd been dreading.

"So, what about your mom?" she said, studying me out of the corner of her eye. "Are your parents, um, divorced?"

I felt the question just where I knew I would, in my throat and stomach. I wanted to say something real, because we'd just been in the big barn and I still had that quiet feeling, deep down inside. But I knew I couldn't go into the whole thing, because my eyes were already swimming, so I looked off toward the farmhouse and gave her what I could.

"They're still married," I began, then told her the story about how they used to say their vows when we were snuggled up on the sofa, the three of us, eating popcorn and watching some late, late movie after they thought I'd fallen asleep. They were sappy and silly that way, and I'll bet no two people ever loved each other the way they did. "The truth is,"

I said, with that picture still hanging there in my mind, "one day she walked out the door, and I never saw her again."

"Oh, Melanie," Leanne breathed, and I looked over to see her blue eyes swimming too. "I don't know what to say."

But she didn't need to say anything. It was even more than I'd told Sabrina, because although Sabrina was always there when I needed her most, it was hard to get around all the stories that we told. We'd never had a moment that felt like this, with Leanne sitting next to me, tears in her eyes.

By the time we headed home, it was late afternoon.

"Thank you!" Leanne and I shouted as Roxie backed out of the drive after dropping us off. We felt happy and tired after spending the day out in the hay and sunshine, with fresh air blowing over the fields. I hardly recognized Leanne with her windblown hair and rosy cheeks.

I could see she didn't want it to end.

"Do you want to do something else?" she said, even though it was almost suppertime, and I figured her parents wouldn't want her staying to dinner. Besides, clouds had gathered while we were driving home, and big drops were starting to fall.

But I guess at that moment, I didn't care.

We went inside to make some macaroni and cheese—with real cheddar. Mom hates the fake stuff. If the package says cheese *food*, just to be reassuring, it's best to take a pass.

The rain was coming down in buckets when we came back out onto the porch.

"Have you ever played Robinson Crusoe?" I said, even though she couldn't have since I'd made up the game myself. I had discovered that if you plug up the street drain with leaves, in no time at all the intersection of Rosemary and Spruce becomes a giant lagoon.

"I'm not sure my mom would like that," she said after I'd explained, but already, I could see the wheels turning. A downpour is irresistible.

"I'll let you borrow some mucky clothes," I said, and then we both ran inside to change.

## FIFTEEN
# *Little Miss Sunshine*

"No, no, Colin, absolutely not! The hook is not to be used for excavating the furniture!"

Miss Gorman had her hands full. Sabrina and I were watching from the fifth row because they were running the opening scene from Act Two, which is all about the pirates, Indians, and lost boys. I felt funny saying Indians, even in my head, when I knew Native Americans was more respectful. These were the things you learned in experimental schools.

"Scalp him, oho, velly quick!" Panther said, and followed Tiger Lily across the stage, hunched over like someone was riding on his back.

Mr. Barrie must not have been thinking about cultural sensitivity when he wrote his play.

"Ugh, ugh, wah!" the other braves cried, leaping around.

"*Peter Pan* isn't quite what I expected," Sabrina said.

I had to agree that parts of it seemed downright awful. It wasn't the way I remembered it, maybe because Mom's voice made everything feel like home. We'd decided that going to Neverland must be even better than Africa or Istanbul because it was everlasting, with fixed stars that shone like pinpricks in the dome of the sky. But it seemed like the story had changed since then, even though it was probably just me.

"Why do the Indians seem so dopey?" Sabrina asked. She'd turned up, back at school, the Monday after my trip to the farm, and we'd fallen right back into our old ways.

"Native Americans," I corrected her. "You have to remember, it was a product of its time," I added, using the exact same words Miss Gorman had when Jeannie Packer complained. Jeannie's great-grandma was full-blooded Sioux, which made everyone jealous because most of us don't know where we came from.

Miss Gorman's words felt strange on my lips. Did she mean that, just because people thought that way, it made it okay?

"Hmm," Sabrina said, and I could tell she wasn't buying it either. "And how come nobody really wants to be in Neverland? I mean, the lost boys only end up there because they fall out of their prams, sort of like a punishment. Peter doesn't seem happy. Everyone just wants a mother, even the pirates."

I had noticed this too, but I didn't really want to talk about it.

"It's complicated," I said, which I had noticed was often enough to end a conversation.

"Hmm," she said again. She sat a moment, then turned to me with a flick of her dark hair. "So, tell me about the postcard."

I went through it all again, how it had been done in Peter Pan code, and how I'd written back to convince Mom to let me join her. I left out my suspicion that Mom might just be humoring me. Sabrina is skeptical enough all on her own.

"Why wait? Now that you have her address, we could just go," she said, but I rolled my eyes.

"We've already been through this. We don't know anything about what we'd be walking into, Sabrina. These are gang members." Somehow, Sabrina had managed to forget all her fears. "Besides," I added, "We can't just barge in on her when she's not expecting us."

"Boys, boys, please don't put those mermaid tails on your heads!" Miss Gorman cried, putting down her script to march up on the stage. "You're going to injure yourselves or others!"

The scene was wrapping up, so I figured I should be heading backstage.

"Look, we'll talk about this later," I said. "Don't you have some props to schlep?"

Sabrina clutched her arm rests and rolled her head back to look at the ceiling.

"If I never see another Dixie cup for the rest of my life, it will be too soon."

I chuckled at that one. One of Sabrina's glamorous duties was running water to various cast members.

"Not everyone can be a star," I said, then laughed as she elbowed me out of my seat.

"Okay, boys, we're going to leave the props out of it for now," Miss Gorman cried. "Please give your cutlasses to Leanne and we'll finish the scene without them."

Sabrina and I were still giggling when we reached the stage.

I touched Miss Gorman's sleeve, and she turned, wilting at the sight of us. "Oh, thank goodness," she said. "Perfect timing, Melanie. You're on."

Things started out well enough.

"Wendy, with an arrow in her heart!" I knelt over Karen as she lay on the stage. "Wendy is dead!"

Perhaps I said it with a bit too much zest, because Karen cocked one eye open and spit on my cheek, just a bit so that no one would know.

"I thought it was only flowers that die," Curly said, which just went to show you how dim the lost boys became in Neverland. That was another thing I'd noticed, how nobody seemed able to keep a thought in his head once he'd hit the magic isle.

"Perhaps she is frightened at being dead," I said, putting some menace into it, but Karen just made a scoffing noise and lay there looking smug. "Whose arrow?" I turned to Tootles.

The lost boys and I went through our shtick, but somehow, my heart just wasn't in it today. Wendy turned out not to be dead, and we built a house around her to keep out the cold while she got better. It was up to Tinker Bell to keep on hating Wendy, flitting around and shooting daggers for looks. We ended the scene by knocking on the door of the house we'd slapped together with a few planks of plywood, and Wendy agreed to be our mother, just before two sides of the house fell down.

"Leanne, will you make a note to see Mr. Olford about the house? I think we need to tinker with the joinery."

I looked over to see Leanne scribbling away on her clipboard. She glanced up and gave me a smile, but I couldn't help noticing that she watched Karen while she did it, out of the corner of her eye.

"I suppose we should run the fight scene," Miss Gorman said, doubtfully. "Remember, no props!"

I was in this scene too, so I crouched behind a paper-mache rock, ready to deliver my line. I had to listen for a while as Hook and Smee hatched their plan to kidnap Wendy and force her to be their own mother. By the time I leapt out, my legs were all tingly.

"Well, then, I am Peter Pan!" I cried.

"Pan!" Colin bellowed, brandishing his hookless hand. "Into the water, Smee. Starkey, mind the boat. Take him dead or alive!"

"Boys, lam into the pirates!" I called, and the melee began, pirate on lost boy, dodging mock blows, then everyone going at it without even knowing who they were smacking. I worked my way up the big rock with Hook in my sights, but it was hard to focus because Karen was watching from the wings, standing right next to Leanne, pointing at me and laughing. I could tell she was saying all sorts of mean things while Leanne just stood there, her clipboard pressed up against her chest. I was just at the part where I was supposed to give Hook a break out of chivalry and then tumble out of sight when I slipped, being so distracted and all, and down I went, bumping right down to land on the stage like I was Moe in the *Three Stooges* instead of the boy who could fly.

"Oh, Melanie, are you okay?" Miss Gorman rushed onto the stage.

Karen was laughing her head off with Kim, who was still in her leotard, her tail slung over her arm.

She must have been the ugliest mermaid ever to flip her fins, what with those two rolls of hair smushing her long, narrow face, but that was small consolation.

"I — I'm okay." I struggled onto one knee, then onto my feet. It was just a few bruises, but I wanted to cry.

Miss Gorman was walking around me, smoothing my clothes, when Karen came up, arms crossed over her chest, like she was holding in the giggles.

"*Poor* Melanie" she oozed. "I've been meaning to tell you how much I like your hair. It looks just like a boy's. So authentic."

Miss Gorman shot her a look, and I realized she had Karen's number, after all.

"Alright kids, take your marks," she said, like she'd decided it was best to downplay the whole thing.

Have I said that I love Miss Gorman?

Karen and I had to run the rest of the scene together, which featured us stuck on a sandbar, just the two of us, with me wounded so I couldn't fly. The water rose as we debated who should grab hold of a kite that happened to be drifting by.

"I won't go without you," Karen said, exactly like a stick with vocal cords. "Let us draw lots to see which is to stay behind."

"And you a lady, never!" I replied, with what gallantry I could muster. I thrust her hands up to grab the kite string. "Ready, Wendy!" I cried as she pretended to float up and away.

I was finally in character, all alone on the stage with the water rising over the rock, lapping at my feet. Soon, I would go under, and it would all be over, but I didn't know why it should hit me so hard, maybe because I was still remembering that tumble and how Leanne had stood there while Karen laughed. It helped a little, lying on a sandbar in Neverland with the mermaids starting to sing, calling the moon to rise. And I knew Peter was supposed to feel fear at last, just like a real boy, because this was it, *the end*. But all I could feel was how sad I was deep down in my bones.

"To die will be an awfully big adventure," I managed, and the words felt strange on my lips, like they'd been pasted on. Then, I saw the bird's nest that was to be my salvation, with its two great eggs that I rolled aside. I climbed into the makeshift raft, then tacked off for the horizon.

"Scene!" Miss Gorman cried, wiping away a tear. I didn't trust myself to talk, so I pretended I needed to take a water break.

Sabrina had an elbow on the water cooler and was holding out a cup as I walked up.

"You're a sight for sore eyes," I said.

"What doesn't kill you makes you stronger," she replied with a wink.

"Mel-an-ie!" Karen sang, all sickly-sweet as she came up from behind. I was feeling pretty raw, and I didn't want to completely lose it, not in front of her. She threw an arm around my shoulder and cinched my head in close, which must have looked friendly enough from a distance, but I could hardly breathe with my mouth pressed up against her T-shirt.

"You really must be more careful," she whined. "Hey, Leanne, aren't you concerned for Melanie's welfare?"

I tried to pry my head sideways for a look, but Karen's hug had become a full-on headlock, and all I could see were the folds of her shirt. The reek of Love's Baby Soft perfume filled my nostrils. I wracked my brain for something to say, feeling the shame of it all and expecting that Sabrina would come to my rescue with a great one-liner, any time now, a real zinger that would put Karen in her place.

"Um, could you please let her go?" said a soft voice, cracking on the last word.

Karen's grip slackened, from shock no doubt, enough for me wriggle free.

"*What* did you say?"

It took a moment for my eyes to refocus after being part of Karen's polyester sandwich. There was Leanne with her big Bambi eyes, clutching the clipboard to her chest, while behind her, Sabrina looked on in amazement.

Leanne cleared her throat. "The play code we all signed says we need to respect each other's personal space," she went on, her voice still thin, but steady.

"Listen, little miss sunshine," Karen began, planting two fists on her hips, "If I need someone to tell me what to—"

"Kids," Miss Gorman called from somewhere behind the curtain, out on the stage. "Let's gather up! It's time for closing circle."

The world seemed to hang in the balance. It was like that moment in old newsreels after a nuclear bomb detonates somewhere in the desert, but before the mushroom cloud sprouts. Karen glared at Leanne like it was World War III, then suddenly leaned into one hip and gave her a smile that had nothing to do with the look in her eye.

"It's okay, Lee Lee," she said, using her stupid little pet name. "You're just doing your job." And then she turned on her heel and flounced away.

Leanne stared at me wide-eyed. I could tell she wasn't sure if what had just happened was a blow for freedom or a death knell. Behind her, Sabrina was still leaning on the water cooler, her head cocked to one side as if she were considering new evidence on a tricky case.

"We better get out there," I said. I risked a smile, then added, "I wouldn't want to get in trouble with the stage manager." Leanne's frightened little face finally broke into a grin.

## SIXTEEN
# *Test Drive*

I had plenty to think about the following Saturday morning, so I figured it was time for a bike ride. Change was in the air, what with Leanne sticking up for me in front of Karen, but I could see she didn't know what to do with this new chutzpah of hers, as if it were a gift from some crazy aunt—confusing to operate and possibly dangerous.

Suddenly, I wished I could talk to Mom about it. The anniversary of her disappearance had been bugging me, looming on the horizon, like back in the days when they thought you could sail right over the edge of the world. It seemed like the better things got, the more I needed her, when you would think it would be just the opposite.

I was just climbing onto my bike seat when I realized I hadn't checked the mailbox yesterday. Dad never checked it, so whatever was in there was just waiting to be seen. I flipped the kickstand down and hustled back for a look-see. There it was—my second postcard!

*Dear Nate Prep,* it read, *if only there were enough pixie dust in the world. I want to believe your words, but what if there's an Indian raid? What if the pirates attack? How could I bear it if you flew away and never came home? Better that I come to you. Perhaps I can devise some magic and be there, in the shadows, when you take flight.* It was signed, *Yours everlastingly, Lily Tiger.*

I was so breathless by the time I finished reading that I almost keeled over. Sure, it was possible she was still humoring me, but her meaning seemed as plain as day. She was too worried about my safety to let me come to her, but she was going to do her level best to come see me on opening night!

And then? Who knew? Maybe she and Dad would patch things up. Maybe she'd give up her dream and let someone else rescue those poor inner-city kids. I mean, I felt for them, but I needed her more. If I closed my eyes and imagined with all my might, I could almost see her out in the last row, about where Sabrina had performed her crazy antics—my mom, wrapped in a scarf to hide her beautiful face.

When I opened my eyes, there was Gloria, looking at me like we were late for an appointment with the shrink.

"Just the person I wanted to see," she said.

I slipped the postcard into my back pocket, lickety-split. I scanned the street behind her, but I couldn't see Gloria's orange Nova anywhere, so I figured she must have parked up the street out of sight. That was sneaky.

"How's tricks?" she said, pretending to have a chipper nature as she tugged down her pantsuit. She has a variety of these suits in velvety, bright colors, and she wears them with gold or silver tennis shoes, depending on her mood. "Thought you might be up with the birds. I'm going to take you for a hike."

This was a strange proposition. I've heard it said that a weed is just a plant growing in the wrong place, and that was how Gloria felt about nature in general.

"Wouldn't you rather go to the mall?" I said, thinking we could walk there, what with Gloria's comfortable shoes.

But I knew it was a test.

"What you need is some Grandma time," she said, dodging my question. "Go park that bike and let's hop in the car."

Once again, I felt a jolt of fear. I had managed okay in Roxie's truck, but driving with Gloria was another matter. How could I beg off without buying myself a one-way ticket to the shrink.

"Okay, I'll be right back."

I went inside to leave Dad a note, but he was already up, fiddling around with the small brush in his jammies. I thought he might give me an out, seeing how we was still sore at Gloria, but he didn't even crack a smile when I told him she wanted to abduct me for the purpose of a forced march in the hinterlands.

"Have fun, Moo Moo," he said, without looking up. The small brush takes all his attention, and besides, the painting was almost finished. He gets a little ditsy toward the end of things. I don't know how he can say goodbye to his creations after they've spent so much time together, selling them off like they're strangers. That can't be easy.

"Bye, then," I said, my last hope gone.

When I came around the hedge, Gloria was leaning against the car, arms folded over her ample chest. Her Nova is pretty slick, if you like that kind of thing. She keeps the paint job glossy, and even the fancy whitewall tires are always clean.

"Climb in," she said, giving her hair a fluff with one hand before easing into the driver's seat.

I closed the passenger-side door gently, but Gloria slammed hers shut with a will. The sound made me jump, and my heart started racing.

"Are you sure you don't want to just walk to the mall? We could test perfumes."

I thought this might prove irresistible, but she just pressed in the clutch and turned the key in the ignition.

"Fasten your seat belt," she said, as if I hadn't done that the moment I got in.

I know it's kooky that I'm afraid of driving. That's what Sabrina would say, but not everything in life is rational. Some things get gummed up inside you, like gunk down a drain if you don't clean it out every now and again. Then, I realized I was making Gloria's case for her, and at this rate I'd end up on the psychiatrist's couch for sure.

"So, have you started a new exercise program?" I said, to distract myself. The answer to this question was usually yes. My heart was hammering so hard, I was afraid I would have a heart attack.

Gloria was fluffing her hair again with only one hand on the wheel. Her hairdo sits on her head in tight, frosted curls, like a poodle that's hanging on for dear life. She rolled down her window, working the handle quick, and yelled at a police car that was speeding by.

"Thanks, Sheriff, for setting an example!"

I wanted to sink into the vinyl seat. Nothing gets under Gloria's skin like authority figures, lording it over us regular folks.

"Piss ant," she grumbled. Gloria doesn't believe in shielding children from colorful language.

This diversion had taken my mind off the drive, but now we were headed out of city limits and picking up speed.

"Talk to me," Gloria said as I clutched my seat with both hands. "I want to hear what's going on in that freckled little head of yours."

It was kind of sweet, Gloria taking me out. She'd never been that kind of grandma.

"I'm in a play," I said. "Did Dad tell you about that?"

*"You* tell me," she said. "Artists are terrible at explaining things."

So I told her about Neverland. At first, I kept things pretty close to my chest because I thought any minute she'd change her mind about being interested. But before I knew it, I was hamming it up almost like I was up there on the stage. I guess it helped take my mind off my mortal peril. Gloria nodded and made the right kind of noises, which she'd never bothered to do before. She generally looked on childhood as a bad habit to be stamped out wherever possible.

We pulled into the Maple Creek Wildlife Refuge and parked in the shade. I let out the breath I'd been holding for the last mile or two.

"Ah, fresh air," Gloria said as we climbed out, arching her back and snaking her arms out to the sides.

All of a sudden, I didn't care if Gloria was faking every minute of it. I was glad I'd come. She smiled at me, and I thought about Dad's theory on the beauty of aging, wondering how I'd missed it when it was right there on Gloria's face.

"Can we go see the frogs?" I said. There was a pond about a half mile up the trail, all grown over with lily pads and sedge grass. The skeeter bugs would scoot across the surface like they had nothing better to do.

"Sure," she said, and I could almost believe she wasn't bored stiff.

Was it possible that Gloria actually loved me? Why else would she lie so much?

"I never took your mom out to places like this," she said, as we started walking. I felt myself stiffen but tried not to let it show.

"She loves to hike," I said.

Gloria looked at me sidelong like she was about to say something, then decided against it. "She didn't get that from me," she said, instead, "and she didn't get it from Harold either."

Harold was her first husband, and she'd already outlived her second, Maurice, the one who left her so much money. Mom never knew her real father, who was just some guy Gloria knew in high school.

"You know, you look a little like your mom," she said, and I couldn't believe my ears. Mom has long, dark hair that she wears up in a messy bun with big, silver hoops in her ears. She wears these small, bright scarves, tied off to the side like an airline stewardess, and I knew she had style because of the way the girls at my old school would look at her, when their mothers only wore sweater sets and polyester pants.

"Do you think so?"

I figured she was buttering me up, maybe thinking that was the best way to get me on the couch. The truth is, I'm scrawny and my hair is limp, at least when it's not cut like a boy's.

"Just you wait till high school," she said with a wink. "You will *bloom*."

That was a nice thought, because I didn't spend much time dwelling on the future, and when I did, I found it sad. I'd wonder what it would be like when I no longer wanted to read books from the children's section of the library, or when I'd want a boy to ask me to dance without it feeling creepy. But the way Gloria said it, it all seemed okay.

"Those critters are something," she said, watching the skeeter bugs cruise across the surface of the water like little boatmen. "How come I never noticed these things before?"

I wanted to grab her hand, but I just couldn't do it. All those years of thinking Gloria didn't like me were like bricks in a wall, real as day even though nobody could see it. I wanted to ask her about Leanne too, and what I should do, but the fact that Gloria wasn't my mom made everything hurt—my stomach and my heart and especially my throat.

We headed back to the car after walking for another mile. Spring was coming on hard. Pollen floated in the air like pixie dust, and all the trees were breaking out with their first bright green leaves.

"Can we come here again some time?" I said, without really thinking. Gloria stopped, smack in the middle of the trail.

She looked down and cupped my chin in her hand again while her eyes misted over. That scared me because I didn't even know she could cry. She must have missed Mom too, I realized, no matter how much makeup she slapped on to hide it.

"Any time you want, darlin'," she said.

The ride home was a bit of a white knuckler, but I got through it okay. I felt like I'd seen a side of Gloria's soul that I was ashamed to have missed. I still didn't quite trust her because I knew she was still fixing to send me to the shrink, who might even dope me up if he didn't like my style.

"See you, sweetie," Gloria said when I hopped out. It was just after ten, and I had the whole day ahead of me. I turned up the walk and decided I'd take a good, long bike ride after all to think things through. The morning had rattled me, and now I was wondering if there was anything else I'd gotten wrong.

## SEVENTEEN
# *Conscientious Objections*

Maybe it was Gloria's visit that got me feeling like I was tired of flying blind. *Flying blind* is an idiom. I use a lot of those. Idioms are sayings that have been around so long, nobody cares whether they make sense. I picked up most of mine from reading books. I was explaining this to Leanne after school because Miss Gorman had been talking about idioms in class that day, and Leanne was confused.

"So, an idiom is kind of like a metaphor?" Leanne said as we sat in my backyard, leaning against the oak tree with our homework spread out around us.

"They can be metaphors, sure," I said. "I guess they're like figurative language because they make you think of two things at once."

I was focusing so hard on explaining what I meant that Leanne's next words caught me by surprise.

"You should be a teacher, Mel," she said.

I blushed. "Oh, thanks," I mumbled, and the box inside me, where I sometimes put our friendship for safekeeping, opened a crack. I've found I can put other people in boxes too, and set them to the side, just like I do with myself. "I really love words," I added, just for something to say.

We were skirting a subject I'd been mulling over for a while. Since I'd cracked open our friendship box a little bit, I decided it was time to talk.

"Remember when you told me that you didn't know why Karen was so mean to me, but maybe it was because she was jealous?"

Leanne looked away. Whenever the subject of Karen comes up, she starts to look trapped, like a cute little rodent that has gotten stuck down a drainpipe.

"Yeah," she said. "I think I remember that."

"What did you mean? Why would Karen be jealous of me?"

Leanne's eyes shot up to my face, as if the answer was obvious.

"Well . . . you know, because . . . because . . . you're *you*." Words are not her strong suit.

"But what is it about me that would make her feel jealous?" I asked. "She's the one with all the friends and the nice clothes and everything. What do *I* do but sit in the tube all day?"

Leanne gave a little laugh. "But Mel, you're . . . *you*," she said again, swishing her hands around as if that would help. "And I guess, well, everyone else is like . . . like . . . everybody else."

"You mean, she's jealous because I'm different?" I tried, but Leanne shook her head.

"No, no, I . . . I'm not saying this very well, am I?" She gave me a shy smile that nudged open the friendship box a little more. "I mean, you *are* different, but you're just like yourself, when everyone is trying not to be."

"Like themselves," I said, and this time she nodded.

"And you seem to like being yourself, even when it's hard," Leanne said, gaining steam, "and I don't think Karen does. Like being herself, I mean."

I felt my blush go deep this time. This was way more than I had ever expected Leanne to notice, and I felt bad all over again for underestimating her, just like I'd done with Gloria. And on top of that, what she said was true. I did like being myself. And on the very top, like a weirdly unappetizing cherry, was the idea that Karen might have enough going on inside that mulish head of hers to envy that.

"Do you really think so?" I said, shaking my head in disbelief.

"I do," Leanne said. "And, well, let's just say people aren't always the way they seem."

I knew this too, and the fact that I'd never thought about it in Karen's case made me so ashamed, I wanted to talk about something else. I thought about thanking Leanne for sticking up for me that day, but I was afraid of what she'd say. So we went back to idioms until it was time for dinner, and then Leanne went on her way.

"Why do you think people hate each other so much?" I asked Roland a few days later as we were sitting in the side yard. It was Friday afternoon, and he'd come by to shoot the breeze with Dad, but he and I ended up talking instead. *Shooting the breeze* is a funny idiom to use in Roland's case because he got paralyzed by stray gunshot in the Vietnam War. "Why do people fight?" I asked, figuring he was uniquely qualified on the subject.

Roland gave his blazer a tug, then pushed himself up on his elbows to adjust his bottom in the chair. He'd come straight from the college and was wearing one of his tweedy blazers with the leather elbow patches.

"That's one for the committee, Schmitty," he said, absentmindedly. Roland talks nonsense when he's thinking. "Are we speaking of someone in particular?"

"No, just in general," I said, because I didn't want to talk about Karen just then.

He rested one elbow on his armrest, pressing a finger into his chin.

"Well, sometimes you fight because you don't have any choice," he said, and I figured he was talking about himself. "Your dad and I were in college during the draft, and back then they didn't make college boys go to war. I didn't think that was fair, so I signed myself up."

This was more than I'd ever heard Roland say about Vietnam. I was surprised because I'd always thought he was drafted.

"But you just said you didn't have a choice," I said, and he pondered for a minute more in his professor kind of way.

"Have you ever heard of a conscientious objector?" he asked. I told him I knew all about the Quakers and the other folks who refused to fight in wars on account of their beliefs. "My conscience was telling me that if there was going to be a war, it shouldn't be only poor boys who had to fight it. And we're all slaves to conscience, whether we ignore it or not."

I noticed that Roland wasn't full of his usual sideways comments, that he was just talking plain, like we understood each other. I sat a little straighter to show him I was up to it because it struck me, for the very first time, that Roland was someone to admire.

"Do you ever regret it?" I asked and hoped I hadn't gone too far. We all knew what it had cost Roland to come home in that wheelchair.

"I'd regret it more if I hadn't gone," he said with one of his lopsided smiles. "I'd regret not living with the choice I made, because you're right, we always have a choice, even if we only have one option."

That was one for the notebook. How could you make a choice if you only had one option? But I'd save that for later. I could tell the serious part was over, and Roland was getting into one of his silly moods.

"Me thinks the lady doth ingest too much," he said when I took a swig off my soda. "How about a little jig?"

So I hopped up to put on some Leon Russell.

Roland and Leanne had me thinking so hard, I thought I'd have an aneurysm. That's what doctors call it when your brain goes kaput. I knew I had a conscience when it came to Karen too, only I wasn't sure how to be nice to someone who wanted to use your intestines for a game of Chinese jump rope.

I was still thinking about it when Miss Gorman announced another big surprise.

"Kids, I'd like you to meet Jane." She stood up on the stage beside a piano that had been wheeled in from the wings. A large, comfortable-looking woman was sitting at the keys, looking over her shoulder and smiling. "Jane is a professional voice coach."

That sounded impressive, and I could feel a ripple go through the ranks.

"She's also a friend of mine," Miss Gorman went on, "so she's agreed to work with us on our vocal technique."

I was all for it. Sabrina nodded approvingly, sitting beside me in the fifth row where we liked to hang out behind everyone else. I was glad we were in agreement, because things had been tense between us, lately.

Jane got to her feet with a little grunt that slipped out. She was even bigger than I'd realized, with a pretty face and skin that looked like a baby's, even though she must have been at least thirty.

"Can anyone tell me how you breathe?" she said. It was such a strange question that even Colin and Davis were quiet. She put a hand on her stomach and sucked in some air, letting her hand rise. "Try that. Feel your hand come up as you breathe in. That's your diaphragm. It's where you want to sing from, not way up here in your chest."

The next hour was fascinating. We took turns coming up on stage to run through scales, singing *do, re, mi*, just like we were the Von Trapp kids from *The Sound of Music*. When my turn came, I felt a little knock-kneed, but Jane was so friendly, smiling over her shoulder and nodding as she played along, that you couldn't help but shine.

"That's it. You have a beautiful range," she said when I went as high as I could go. "When you get to the high notes, try to imagine that your voice is in your head."

Now she was speaking my language. I imagined for all I was worth, and suddenly it was like a switch got flipped inside me, and my voice got louder, filling up my head like helium in a balloon. I sounded even better than I did in the shower.

"Excellent!" Jane smiled.

"Thanks!" I said back and exited the stage. I couldn't call her Miss Anything because I didn't know her last name, so I left it at that.

"That was great, Mel!" Leanne said, turning around in her seat when I got back to mine. I must have done *really* well for her to forget herself, even with Karen sitting beside her, ogling her all wide-eyed like her ocular condition was acting up. Ever since Leanne stood up to her, Karen had tightened the reins.

I was feeling fluttery and like I might have a stupid smile on my face, so I looked over at Sabrina for a check-in.

"Hmm," she said, which was typical. I guess she didn't like how Leanne still sat next to Karen, and I could see her point.

Ever since I'd let some light into our friendship box, I'd been trying to feel okay about how things stood between Leanne and me. I could see she was trying to be brave, but maybe the idea of Karen turning on her was just too much to take. She wasn't the type to just hide out in the tube, so she'd chosen to live by that age-old adage, keep your friends close, but your enemies closer.

If only I could get Karen to lighten up, maybe Leanne and I could be school friends too. Sabrina stared me down for a few minutes, her dark, straight hair framing her face, and I felt like she was reading my mind, thinking I was a pushover.

Then, she smiled and said, "But you sang really well."

Davis was at the piano, exploring his lower range, not listening to a word Jane said.

"Hooow looow caaan yooou goooooo," he sang, going down a step each time until his voice was just a rumble.

Everyone wanted to sing with Jane, so we sat there for what seemed like hours. By the time we got outside, lots of the parents were waiting to pick their kids up, some leaning against their cars, a few jawing with each other about whatever it is parents discuss. I live close to school and can walk home even when it's almost dark. I was strolling out through the parking lot when all of a sudden I heard this growl, like a bear, and turned.

"*What* did you say?" the voice said.

There stood the hugest man I'd ever seen. He must have been over six feet tall, and he was built like a bear too, towering over some little kid who only reached up to my knee, which isn't saying much, because I'm a shrimp.

"She said ouch because you stepped on her toe!" Karen said. I hadn't even noticed her until she stepped up and set her jaw so that she and the bear-man were scowling face to face. Then he did something that made me feel sick inside.

He slapped Karen right up the side of her head, so hard she had to bend over for a minute, holding her head with one hand.

At first, I thought I should run for help because some criminal had escaped from the state penitentiary and was roaming the streets at will, roughing up little kids. Then I saw them all get into a beat-up Chevy and drive off—the man, the little kid, and Karen—all bumping out of the parking lot, looking in different directions out the windows. When I wrote in my notebook that everyone has a story, even Karen, I wasn't thinking that she really *had* a mean dad. And now I saw it was even worse, because he was mean way down deep inside, and that changed everything.

I couldn't help it. I felt sorry for Karen, the way you feel sorry for a poor orphaned mountain lion, right before it bites off your hand.

My conscience was talking up a storm after that, yammering all the way home. I knew with a sinking feeling that there was nothing else for it but to try. If I could just make Karen feel good about herself, maybe she'd stop bugging me. Even better, maybe it wouldn't be so bad for her, living with a grizzly for a dad. If you had something of your own, you could put up with almost anything. I knew that to be true because, between the squirrels and my postcards and my two new friends, I'd done it myself. And as crazy as it sounds, I wanted to do something nice for Karen.

The question was, what? And how on earth could I ever get her to let me?

## EIGHTEEN
# *The Everything Around Us*

The next week was fun, and I thought things might be looking up for me. Jane came to homeroom and taught us some songs from *The Muppet Movie*, which we sang a cappella, without any accompaniment. We all sat on our desks, side by side, our voices blending together until you couldn't tell who was who. Even Karen was enjoying it, only she couldn't keep her voice from sticking out. Some things just go against a person's grain, and you could see it was like splinters under her fingernails every time Jane looked over and pressed down on the air with her palm, like she was trying to close a lid.

That got me thinking. Would Karen let me help her learn to sing?

I shot the idea down at once, but it kept popping up, just like one of the zombies out of Colin and

Davis's stories. I'd gotten pretty good at singing in a group, hearing everyone around me and feeling a part of things. And I knew it was a matter of imagination, if I could just get Karen to understand what that was. But I also knew she'd never let me help her. So I sat on the idea for a few more days, scooting around every time it popped up to squash it down again, like you do when you're trying to sit on top of a ball in a pool.

Then I remembered how Miss Gorman had gotten me to help Leanne.

Who says no to a teacher? Especially one like Miss Gorman. And even Karen was a sucker for Miss Gorman's unique brand of enthusiasm. Maybe I could get Karen to think it was Miss Gorman's idea.

I was so nervous that Friday after school, I might have wet my pants, just like a kindergartner, if I hadn't already gone to the bathroom twice.

"Hey, Karen, wait up," I called as all the kids were walking away from school, after the bell. I hoped she wouldn't remember that day she'd called out to me, just like this, because then she might think I was getting even. But she only turned and looked at me like I was speaking chimpanzee. "Miss Gorman asked me to ask you something," I blurted. I had prepared a speech, but my brain center was down again, and I couldn't remember a word. "She said maybe we could buddy up for singing practice."

My face must have been bright red because Karen's head tilted to the side as she looked at me. Her eyes narrowed to slits.

"Nice try, Smellanie." She turned to go.

"No, really," I yelped, running around to get right in front of her. "I think it was Miss Jane's idea," I babbled on, "to team people up for moral support."

She squinted again and said, "What do you mean?"

This next part was tricky. I didn't want to set myself up as superior, but I had to make her believe I could help her.

"You know what a bad singer I was, at the audition," I tried, which was kind of true. "Maybe Miss Gorman and Miss Jane thought if *I* could improve, anyone could. And there's nothing like learning something yourself to help you teach someone else."

This idea seemed to grab her, maybe because I was putting myself down. She was still squinting at me, but I could see I'd almost won her over, if I could just keep from messing things up.

"When," she said, like she was in no mood for words. Ever since the episode with her dad, she didn't seem to have the heart for much, even bullying me.

"Oh, um, how about, um," I hemmed and hawed. I hadn't thought I'd get this far. "Tomorrow is Saturday. Let's meet at Swift Park." Neutral territory was best.

"Fine, Smellanie, ten sharp," she said, then breezed past me, knocking me with her shoulder, just in case I thought we were friends.

"Great. Good. See you, then." I stood there, waving behind her when she couldn't even see me. At least Sabrina wasn't around to witness my shame.

The truth was, I felt good as I broke off for home. I was feeling pretty clever, which is usually a bad sign. People often slap themselves on the back right before they fall off a cliff. I was whistling away, like I was the mayor of Fairview, when Sabrina showed up and fell into stride.

I told her my bright idea, thinking I should get it over with.

"How are you going to make her a better singer?" she asked, surprising me. I thought she'd tell me what a dummy I was right off the bat. That's her way of saying she cares.

"Oh, I've got lots of ideas," I said, which was not strictly true. "I'll have her singing like a sparrow."

"Sparrows don't blend in," Sabrina said, and I realized she was right. But when had my imagination ever failed me?

"Don't answer that," I said because I could tell she was reading my mind again.

"Imagination isn't everything," she said as we turned onto Rosemary Street.

Saturday morning I woke up with that pit in my stomach. Even watching the squirrels didn't help, so I got up and roamed around the house, doing the few dishes that were in the sink, taking out the garbage, even wiping out the fridge. Cleaning helps when I've got a lot on my mind.

Dad shuffled out of his main floor bedroom, stretching and yawning, his mess of brown hair sticking out like a little boy's. I had his cup of instant coffee ready to go.

"Here, Dad." I handed him the mug.

"Thanks, Moo Moo." His soft brown eyes lit up. "You're in a chipper mood."

I didn't want to tell him it was just nerves, so we sat at the Formica table in the kitchen and just talked about nothing much. That helped more than cleaning had done, and by the time 9:30 rolled around, I was as ready as I'd ever be.

"I'm going to the park," I said and headed for the back door.

"See you later, alligator," Dad said with a frumpy smile, then shuffled into the living room where I guess he planned to paint in his pajamas.

"After a while, crocodile," I yelled, and hopped on my bike to go.

I took the long way to the park, past the old train station, then down some gravel roads. It wasn't as good as getting lost, but there was no time for that, and I needed to think. I had turned a bunch of ideas over in my head, but I just couldn't figure it out. Would the things that worked for me ever work for someone like Karen?

She was sitting on the swings when I got to Swift Park, lolling around with her feet planted wide.

"'Bout time," she said, even though I had arrived on the dot.

"You ready to get singing?" I asked, angling for a positive note, but she just looked at me like I was a moron. "Right. Okay, I was thinking we could sit over there, under the trees."

The fringes of Swift Park are borderline-forgotten places, and I needed all the help I could get. Maybe some of that magic would seep into Karen without her even knowing it. We sat under the birches, her leaning against a tree, me with my bent knees cradled between my elbows.

"Let's start with your strengths," I said. "It seems like you're . . . um . . . good at projecting."

Karen leaned forward, eyeing me suspiciously.

"What's that supposed to mean," she barked. I guess she's not as dim as she seems.

"No, no, it's a strength, really," I said quickly. "When you're up on stage, all by yourself, it's perfect." Then, inspiration struck. "You're what people call a diva."

She leaned back slowly, picking her teeth with a twig. "What's a diva," she sneered, but I could tell she liked the sound of it.

"A diva is the star of the show in an opera or maybe a Broadway hit," I said. "She's the one who belts out songs so everyone can hear, the one who has a ton of star quality."

I was laying it on pretty thick, but Karen nodded, like that just about summed her up.

"So what do I need lessons from you for?" she said. "Sounds like I should be teaching you."

"Uh huh. Yeah. Well, we can get to that, too. But maybe I can teach you how to be versatile." That was kind of a fancy word, and she bristled, so I rushed on, "Sometimes, you have to sing with other people, like we do with Miss Jane, and then you need to know how to . . . how to . . . um . . . turn down your star quality."

The star quality thing was sheer brilliance. Karen had stopped squinting at me like I was a roach she might smash with her shoe.

"Okay, okay," she said, nodding, "so, how?"

That's when I hit the end of my tether, like a dog on a short leash. There she was, looking at me for the first time as if I were marginally human, and I couldn't think of a thing. I strained this way and that, just like a dog does when you haven't trained him properly, but every direction brought me up short. Then, I noticed a bruise that was fading under Karen's eye. Maybe she'd just fallen off her bike, but it reminded me of that slap upside the head, and before I knew it, words were coming out of my mouth.

"Do you have a safe place?"

Karen's eyes popped open so wide, I could see the white around the iris.

*"What?"*

"I mean, when you just need to think, or be alone, or . . . or feel like you're on your own turf," I rushed on, hoping she wasn't going to hop up and leave. Neither one of us had expected me to get personal.

"What does that have to do with singing?" she said, but she sounded more confused than angry.

"It just does." My heart was pounding in my ears. "And it doesn't have to be a real place. Sometimes I go to places in my head."

I was sure I'd lost her, but my words seemed to have a reverse psychology effect, because she started laughing and said, "That's dopey. My place is real."

"Oh really?" I said. "Tell me about it."

So she did. Her safe place was in the tree house she had built in the back yard with her dad when she was five. I tried to hide my surprise because I knew she hadn't seen me that day in the parking lot, and now I was confused because she seemed so proud of the fact that her dad had helped her.

"It's about fifteen feet up in the tree, not for babies," she said, with a sneer that was meant for me.

Now I had something to work with. We sat under those birches for the next hour while I taught Karen how to go to the tree house in her head and how to use that feeling to make her voice a part of everything around us. That's what happens when you feel safe. You blend in, even while you're shining out.

"Let's try a few bars together," I said, and we sang the first part of *The Rose*, which, as it turns out, was both of our favorite song.

*Not* that we were bonding.

"Not bad, Smellanie," she said when it was time to go. "Monday is the Founder's Day assembly. Perfect place to test out your little tricks."

I realized with a start that she was right. I had forgotten all about the assembly, which happened only once a year.

"Oh, yeah, perfect," I said, swallowing a lump.

"You just better hope they hold up," she said. Then off she went to torture other sentient beings.

Truer words were never said.

# NINETEEN
# *Only Illusions*

"Isn't Jane the best?" Leanne said on Monday as we walked into Mrs. Brandy's room. She sat on one side of me in guitar while Sabrina sat on the other, studying her strings like they were wires on a bomb she was defusing. I could feel her itching to point out that Leanne only sat next to us when Karen wasn't there, but I tried to keep the peace.

Everyone was excited about the Founder's Day assembly, and recess was a riot. Some of us had started rehearsing scenes from *Peter Pan* over by the baseball field, and that helped to pass the time. Opening night was only a couple of weeks away, and by now even Harry knew his lines.

"Har, blow me down, the natives be restless," Colin cried, bursting out of the grove of cottonwoods behind the field and swinging a stick. He and Davis were always rehearsing fight scenes that weren't in the play, with Davis taking the role of Mr. Bill, running around and crooning, "Oh nooooo, Mr. Hands, don't feed me to the croc-o-dile! Oh nooooo, those are my intestines, not spaghetti!"

Sabrina and I were standing in the shadow of the trees, watching the chaos unfold. We'd been talking about the latest postcard from Mom, debating the odds that she'd make it to opening night, when the weirdest thing in the history of the world happened. Kim walked over to us while Karen was in the bathroom. She wasn't wearing any makeup today, which made a nice change, and I noticed that she had a sprinkling of freckles over her nose, like me.

"Hey, Mel," she said, just like we were friends. "Do you think Jane was an opera singer in a former life? My mom says we all have former lives, only you forget them or else it would be too hard to keep track of stuff."

This was exactly the kind of statement that would have had me rolling my eyes if I'd overheard her saying it to Karen, but it sounded different now that she was saying it to me.

"Um, maybe," I said, too surprised to reply with my usual eloquence.

"There's extensive, anecdotal evidence of former lives in most cultures, going back centuries," Sabrina added, sagely. I'm not sure Kim understood all that, but then she smiled, and I saw that one of her permanent teeth was still coming in.

"Well, see you," she said, then hustled off, her tubular curls kind of flapping in her haste, because even Karen can only take so much time in the bathroom.

After that, I was even more keen for my plan to work.

There was so much excitement in the air, it was hard to settle down once we all took our seats in the cafeteria. There's a stage at one end, and with the tables gone and folding chairs set up in rows, it looked just like an auditorium. The real one was full of Neverland stuff, and I guess the powers-that-be just didn't want to deal with that.

The Founders took their special seats, angled off to the side in a row. Folding chairs aren't very grand, but the Founders aren't grand people—more like back-to-the-land types. One of them, Mr. Bowler, came from money before he struck off on his own path, and it was his inheritance that paid the bills when they got the school started. Sometimes I wonder if his parents are rolling over in their graves, wishing he'd spent his cash on fancy stuff, like maybe a strip mall or a miniature golf course.

"Welcome— " Mr. Howard broke off and tapped the mike a few times until it started whining, then Mr. Olford hopped up while we all covered our ears.

"Welcome," he said again, after they'd sorted that out. "Here we are, another year, another chance to plant seeds for tomorrow's crop in the fertile minds of these outstanding students." He went on like that for a while, full of metaphors about Buckminster Fuller's dreams for the future of humanity. That's about as grand as it gets with this crowd. It was right up my alley, but I could hear the other kids fidgeting in their chairs.

Finally, he rolled out the program.

"First up, we have a tableau entitled 'Nature's Bounty.'"

The second graders trooped onto stage, suited up in tree and nymph costumes, then arranged themselves on the taped-off X's. A tableau is an old-fashioned way of making a diorama, only with people for props. They were popular back when men wore suits all the time and ladies had bustles stuck up under their skirts. The second graders stood as still as they could, the trees with their arms out to the side, the nymphs frozen like they'd been caught spying on sleeping maidens. It was a real test, considering how hard it is to sit tight when you're only seven or eight, but they pulled it off, except for little Maisie, who clearly had forgotten to hit the bathroom after recess. I could have coached her on that.

"Next, a game show!" Mr. Howard announced after the second graders were settled back in their seats.

The fourth graders hauled in a makeshift contestant's stand from the wings, and then a stool for the host, Jimmy Schmidt, who's a real ham and was tossing out questions with a corny twang, slapping his thigh when a contestant got the answer right.

"What was this nation's first national park?" he asked the panel, and Jennifer Peal squeezed her buzzer, one of those bike horns with the big, red bulb.

"Yosemite!" she squeaked, but Jimmy looked out to the audience with a knowing shake of the head. He's a natural.

"Tsk tsk. Good guess, little lady, but the answer is Yellowstone. I think we know "*Y*" you got that one wrong!"

It was just the sort of rotten pun a game show host would make, and he said the "little lady" part like he was patting her on the head. Game show hosts are real chauvinists.

That skit was a hard act to follow, and our class was up next. I don't know why I was so nervous. Karen had caught on really well to my singing tips, but as we filed onto stage, I thought I might break into the pee pee dance too, just like Maisie. That's what I got for feeling high and mighty.

"And now, a little music," Mr. Howard said, turning toward us with a sweep of his arm. There we were, standing in two rows, the shorter people up front, and me smack in the middle with Karen right behind. That was lucky since I'd be able to tell firsthand if she was blending in. But it made me nervous too.

We all started singing, and I felt my spirits lift with the music. We sounded way better than Kermit the Frog had when he sang this song in *The Muppet Movie*. Okay, that's not a very high bar, but between Davis holding the base line and Leanne's soprano, we had a real symphonic effect going on.

And there was Karen, looking over my head and cooing like a dove!

She sounded downright seraphic. That's a fancy word that people rarely use in everyday speech unless they're talking about a dopey look on someone's face. It means angelic. I couldn't have been happier, what with that lovely song blowing all around me, so I just gave into it and started to sway.

Before you knew it, we were all swaying, the whole group as one, keeping the beat and sending our notes on up to the sky. The next refrain stepped up in pitch, and you could feel the energy mount. I could tell Karen was extra excited, it being a new experience and all, but I started to wonder if she was enjoying it a little *too* much, As the pitch rose, her tone started to warble and grow. She was letting go alright, but instead of blending into the flock, she seemed to be taking flight.

That's when her voice started to crack.

I had thought that Karen's safe place would smooth out her rough spots, but now I saw that even her smooth spots stuck out. She's just one of those people.

By the time we got to the last refrain, I wasn't the only one who had noticed. Karen must have really soared on the last note, because everyone in the audience was laughing. I think they thought it was all a gag. I couldn't see Karen behind me, but I could *feel* her, looking around, checking out the people to either side, and then drawing the only conclusion possible in the circumstances.

Today, she was the butt of the joke.

Miss Gorman hustled us off stage, but not before Karen started grousing, which just goes to show you how grumpy she was. Usually she puts on her best face for the teachers.

"If you hadn't asked that twerp to share her stupid singing tips with me," she was saying as we all filed down the steps like cows bottle-necked behind a cattle guard.

I cut in front of a few people to hustle back to my seat, but not before I heard Miss Gorman say, "I'm not sure what you mean, Karen. I did nothing of the kind."

I don't remember the rest of the assembly.

I've heard that soldiers experience something called battle fatigue under the pressures of war. Maybe that's what happened to me. I don't remember a thing until I was outside the cafeteria, hurrying through the breezeway. But Karen must have made an end run, because there she was, planted right in front of my locker, arms crossed over her chest.

"That's *it*," she said, sticking a finger hard into my chest twice, once for each word. "You've messed with the wrong Wagner, Smellanie." Wagner is Karen's last name, and I was thinking she was right.

"Karen, you don't understand. I was trying to help, honest. I thought that maybe—"

"Stuff it!" she yelled, real tears in her eyes. "You lied to me!"

I didn't know what to say. She was right, even if I'd told myself I was lying for the right reasons.

"Karen I— I— I'm sorry!" I cried. She was pushing me backwards, one push for each step I took until I was up against a breezeway pillar. Other kids were gathering round, and I knew I was really in for it now, but then Mr. Funkel walked out of the double doors, whistling, and the moment was broken.

"You're finished," Karen hissed, poking me one last time in the chest before stalking away. The other kids milled off, looking over their shoulders like they were half relieved and half sorry all the hubbub was over. I stood there, heaving and blinking back tears until everyone was gone, rubbing the spot on my chest where Karen had poked me.

I had a bad feeling, rising in my gut, that this was the beginning of the end.

# TWENTY
# *Blue*

The next few days were like that part of a made-for-TV movie where sappy music plays and scenes flit by, showing people holding hands and running through fields of poppies. Time is passing, but nothing seems real, and you know that trouble is right around the bend.

But I'm good at pretending.

"I have something to show you," Leanne said after school when we didn't have rehearsal. We were hanging out under the oak tree again because it was such a yummy day. Her cheeks were pink against the usual paleness, so I could tell she was nervous as she sat cross-legged, pulling her backpack into her lap to rummage around. "Here," she said, and pulled out a sheet.

I took it in my hands and held it up to the light.

"Wow," I breathed, softly. "It's beautiful."

Leanne had drawn a picture using just a pencil and eraser. It was her cloud castle, and it was full of little details, like glittery window panes and faces in the billows, all smeared over with careful strokes of the eraser. I didn't even know she could draw. "Maybe *this* is your secret language," I said, half to myself, because every person's soul has a way of talking to the world, if they can only find out what it is.

"I want you to have it," she said, and I knew it was a turning point. We hadn't talked about the blow up with Karen, not with words, but when I looked into her eyes, for a moment I couldn't tell where she ended and I began. And for the first time, I felt like everything might turn out okay.

Then she said something so amazing, I couldn't breathe. "You're my very best friend." She gave my knee a shy little pat.

I hoped I'd said enough to let her know that I would keep her gift forever, the picture she'd made me, and the words she'd said. I worried about it the next morning as I watched the squirrels. She might decide to take it back, thinking I didn't treasure it. But you can't watch squirrels for long and keep worrying, what with all those busy paws handling nuts like there's nothing else worth doing. By the time I got to school, I was back to expecting that everything would be different now, that Leanne was finally going to be my all-the-time friend. What good was a best friend if you only dusted them off after hours? Besides, something had to give—Leanne couldn't keep standing on the sidelines now that Karen had declared full-out war.

Maybe we could sit next to each other in math and history. Then, Sabrina would see I wasn't such a dope after all.

I settled into Mr. Howard's class and got ready for whatever difficult subjects lay in store. I even put my backpack on the desk next to me to save it. It was one of those mornings when everyone is almost late, and it was a real zoo around the doorway. David and Cory got stuck between the door jams, shoulder to shoulder, and then Leanne rushed in with flushed cheeks. She looked over at me and the empty desk, and our eyes locked, so I figured she was about to come over when I heard Karen loud-mouthing about nothing in particular.

"That's what I told him!" she said to Kim, finishing up on whatever they were talking about in the hall. Almost everyone was seated now, and Mr. Howard was already wiping the chalkboard down, but all of a sudden the moment got still and wide, like it does when the whole world is at stake.

Leanne had her mouth half-open and was looking at me with eyes like a startled deer. Karen took the whole thing in at a glance, then sallied up beside

Leanne and threw an arm around her shoulder, staring me down.

"Come on, Lee Lee. Let's sit at the back."

It felt strange, her saying those words to Leanne when we all knew they were meant for me. Leanne was looking at me like she was trying to write a whole book just with her eyes, but still, she didn't move. I guess there are lots of doors in the world, and not all of them lead to Neverland, because she just stood there on the threshold, and none of us knew which one she'd choose.

I counted three heartbeats.

Then, she chose.

"Let me show you my new nail polish," Karen said, extra chummy as they walked on by. "It would look so pretty with your blue eyes."

Sabrina slid into the empty desk beside me just before the bell rang.

"After-school friends," she said, and then we sat there in silence, waiting for class to begin.

After that, Leanne and I both knew it was over. We didn't even try to pretend we were still friends, because it hurt too much. I may have an imagination in a million, but I'm no good at covering up what I really am. And I didn't have the heart to go around as if things were the same, when we both knew where Leanne stood.

"At least you have some self-respect," Sabrina said as we sat in the alley, tossing bits of glass on the big pile. I was dismantling my jewel factory, thinking that might act as a kind of catharsis. Gloria would like that term, and I could always trot it out if we ever got to talking about psychiatric treatment.

"Do we have to talk about this?" I said, nicking my pinky finger.

"I'm just trying to help." Sabrina had taken to dressing like her namesake, and today she was sporting a classy blouse and tan slacks. She was quiet for a moment, and I could feel her studying me, even though I wasn't looking at her directly. "You still have me," she said finally.

That was sweet, and it should have made me feel better. Even though Sabrina and I argue sometimes, she's the most loyal friend I've ever had. And I tried to make it help. After all, why should a person want to be friends with someone who won't stand up for them? And Sabrina always had my back, no matter what. She wanted the best for me, deep down inside—only, that's all there seemed to be, deep down inside her, like she had this hole in the middle of her life that made it hard to feel like I knew her, no matter how much she cared. Maybe all those stories we told each other were like layers of wrapping paper on an empty box.

"What would Sabrina Duncan do?" I asked, leaning back on one elbow and sticking my pinky in my mouth.

Sabrina hugged her knees and squinted off down the alleyway. "Ooh. Are we talking revenge or espionage?"

But that only made me sadder because I couldn't help loving Leanne, even with everything that had happened.

"Never mind," I said, tossing it off like it was no big deal. I pulled my pinky out and dusted off my hands. "I should probably get on home."

Sabrina sized me up with those canny brown eyes and gave a nod.

"I'll just clean up here," she said. "You go on ahead. I'm chipping in for the litter campaign."

Being at home wasn't any better. Dad was out with Roland, having a beer in the park because Roland had just finished grading a whole slew of papers and needed to unwind. That's what the note said, taped to the fridge, but I figured this was just another excuse to get Dad out of the house. As our one-year anniversary date drew near, Roland and Roxie came around more often, cracking jokes while they studied Dad on the sly. Eventually, they'd make it over to hug me or ruffle my hair. I know they love me, but sometimes adults don't seem to understand what kids need, just like Mr. Barrie going through all that trouble to make up Neverland but still not getting it right.

I went up to my room and got out my library bag, laying all the books out, side by side. It was a real gold mine. I narrowed it down to three, *The Diamond in the Window*, *The Egypt Game*, and *Half Magic*. This was going to be hard, but I knew I was facing a long night, so I closed my eyes and mixed them up, picking two at random.

*Half Magic* came in first, with *The Egypt Game* runner-up. I climbed into bed, thinking I could pretend it was a sick day, and that I'd held the thermometer up to the light bulb, just to get a day off without actually feeling bad. Right away, I pegged *Half Magic* as a winner. On any ordinary day, I'd be hooked for the long haul, but I kept shifting around, first to one side, then to the other, like I was on pins and needles, only inside where I couldn't reach. The room was getting darker too, even though the sky was still blue beyond the oak, so I turned on all the lights, hoping to create some cheer.

After twenty minutes, I knew it was no use. My second book had fared no better than the first. I went to put it on my dresser, then caught sight of one of Mom's postcards. And even though I knew better, I couldn't help picking it up for another read.

There was her trick name, Lily Tiger, with all the little x's and o's before it in place of the hugs and kisses she couldn't give me in person. I didn't make a sound, but all of a sudden, my cheeks were so wet there were drops coming off my chin, and my stomach kept convulsing like I had to throw up. I knew that was bad, and I wondered if getting postcards from Mom was such a good idea after all. So I stashed it deep inside my drawer, wondering what a person should do when nothing seemed to work.

Then it hit me — I could make a blanket fort, just like the old days.

I headed for the stairs, wiping my cheeks with the back of my hand. Down in the kitchen, I snagged a few chairs, pulling them into the living room, then throwing an afghan and two quilts over the top. Inside, it was cozy with all the pillows arranged, and the lamp I'd rigged up casting a friendly glow. The whole time, I kept thinking about opening night, picturing Mom in the front row and me up on the stage, the star of the show. It would be like our own little game had grown up for all the world to see. But once I got settled, the fort just felt stuffy and small and not at all like Neverland, except that maybe it was a place without any mothers.

I ripped the quilt aside, like I was starved for air.

The window seat. That was it. I hadn't done that in ages.

First, I needed music, and I knew just the thing. Joni Mitchell is Mom's favorite singer, even though she didn't have too many Top 40 hits. Mom told me Joni Mitchell never tried to be a big star because she only wanted to sound like herself, but she became famous anyway. She has this high, clear voice, fluttering around, and her words paint pictures that don't always make sense.

I put on *Blue* and settled into the window seat with two pillows propped up, like I was snuggling Mom. If I'm honest, that was probably my idea from the start, that the pillows might feel like her when I leaned in, soft and warm. I took the first issue off the stack of magazines while Joni started in, her voice sweet and true, looking for the highest branch. I'd picked *Blue* because, frankly, I was feeling so blue, and I've found that when you're sad it's best to get up close to it. There's no use in wandering off and pretending you're fine when you're not, because then the sadness just gets sadder, straggling behind, all on its own.

I hugged one of the pillows to my stomach, as if I had an arm around Mom's waist, and flipped through the pages. The main article was about starvation in Africa and featured pictures of little kids with basketball bellies and big, sad eyes. If I was out to make myself sadder, I was off to a good start. I punched the pillow a few times, trying to get comfortable, and flipped through to an article about fruit flies, then looked at some women all covered with scarves from head to toe. But the pillow didn't feel like Mom at all, and it didn't smell like her either, and even though I was imagining for all I was worth, it wasn't working.

I wondered, suddenly, if my theory was all wrong. That happens once in a great while. Maybe some sorrows were too big to get up close to, and if you tried, they'd just swallow you whole. I got panicky because now there were sobs in my throat, making it hard to breathe. Then Joni hit some high notes in the minor key, which always makes them seem like they're just dying to get some place they're never going to reach.

That's when I lost it.

I started punching the pillow hard, until feathers came poofing out. It seemed like I might hurt myself, crying like that and punching away, with my insides all bunched up in my throat and my eyes. What if I never stopped crying? What if it never got any better, and there was only an awful longing all the time, an ache you had to live with for the rest of your life, like tennis elbow, only a million times worse?

I got up to my room as fast as I could. I didn't want Dad to come in, because I knew it would scare him to see me that way. He'd probably think Gloria was right, that I'd lost all my marbles and that he'd been a cruddy dad, leaving me to go stick his head into paintings all the time.

By the time I stopped crying, it was all I could do to crawl under the covers and go to sleep.

## TWENTY ONE
# *Unsafe Zone*

The next morning, I lay in bed for a long time watching the squirrels. I felt quiet inside, not happy or sad, just floating around. I felt like I could drift right out the window and join the squirrels as they went about their day. It was sort of like thinking, with that same timeless quality, only different too because my head was empty, except for a few distant points of light that winked in and out, saying, *what's it about, anyway*, and *what's the point of it all?*

I was almost late for school.

"Sure does look like a house I'd like to live in." Mr. Olford said during fourth period.

These were more words than I had ever heard him string together at one time. I was gluing the last few bits of bark onto the birdhouse after having put the project aside for a while. Sabrina and I had been working on props for the play, swords and daggers, but today she was back to cutting school, which just made me more blue. I guess I hadn't been a very good friend to her, lately.

"There's room for two birds," I pointed out, even though I'd shown him before.

"Two birds are better than one," he said, smiling and taking a swig off his mug. His arms were crossed over his belly again, so he just settled the mug back onto his forearm.

"Melanie, *love* the bird's nest," Karen said all the way from her table by the window. In the past few days, she'd gotten bolder, but you'd think she could have come up with some fresh material. Leanne rested her chin on the table as she fiddled with the wheels of her toy car, just like she'd had a lobotomy, which is where doctors take your brain out when they think it's not working right. Problem solved.

I saw now that Leanne was better at pretending than she gave herself credit for.

"Hey, Karen," Kim said, elbowing her friend and holding up her wooden spoon, "do you think I'll get splinters in my lips if I eat with this?"

Karen rolled her eyes and said something out of hearing, but you didn't need x-ray vision to see it go in one of Kim's ears and right out the other. I knew there was more to her than that, but I guess I was just feeling bitter.

Mr. Olford had been looking back and forth between our tables and frowning, which made his nice, easy face look all wrong. He gave me a sad smile, and I could tell he wanted to help. I smiled back, just to show him I'd gotten the message. But we both knew he was no match for Karen, so he just shook his head slowly and wandered back to his safe zone.

This was my life now, and rehearsal wasn't much better.

The lost boys were lounging on the stage while Karen sat on a stump in her frilly, white nightgown and told them a story. It was a true story, about the life Wendy had left behind, but since even true stuff is made up in Neverland, the lost boys were eating it up.

"So all the children flew away," she said. "They flew away to Neverland where the lost boys are."

I knelt at stage right, play-whittling some reed pipes. Just off stage, Leanne was scribbling like mad on her clipboard, maybe drawing another picture.

"I just *thought* they did," said Curly, who was played by a fourth grader named Roy. "I don't know how it is, but I just thought they did," he said, and I felt sorry for the lost boys all over again. How did they get through the day without eating their own tongues?

"Oh, Wendy," said Tootles, "was one of the lost boys called Tootles?"

This went on for a while with the lost boys asking what their belly buttons were for and how come their noses were on the front of their faces and not behind their ears.

"A little less noise there," I said, but my line came out a kind of cranky.

Now Wendy was at the part that was supposed to get my attention.

"But our heroine knew that her mother would always leave the window open for her progeny to fly back by," she said, "so they stayed away for years and had a lovely time."

Maybe it was just my bad night in the window seat, but I'd had it with all the talk about mothers, with everyone either wanting one or not and being all confused about it.

Wendy went on to describe how they'd fly back to London when they were old and fat, my cue to groan.

"Peter, what is it?" She ran over to my side. "Where is it?" she added, prodding my chest a bit too thoroughly.

"It isn't that kind of pain," I said, scooting out of reach. "Wendy, you are wrong about mothers. I thought like you about the window, so I stayed away for moons and moons, and then I flew back, but the window was barred, for my mother had forgotten all about me and there was another little boy sleeping in my bed."

I could barely get the words past the lump in my throat. Hopefully, Karen would just think I was a great actor.

But sharks are an ancient species.

"Are you sure mothers are like that?" she said, studying my face as if she were looking for an angle. She was confused for the moment, but in the case of sharks, instinct makes up for the lack of a large frontal lobe.

"Yes," I squeaked.

Somehow, I made it through the rest of the scene, with Karen eyeing me suspiciously the whole time. Blood was blood, and she knew something was up, but what? And how could she use it to disembowel me completely?

"Scene!" Miss Gorman cried. "Ten-minute break. Remember to flush those toilets," she said, putting a hand on Colin's and Davis's heads. "Leave it better than you found it, that's the Buckminster way."

I headed for the third row and found that Sabrina had come back after all.

"Where were you all day," I said, still fighting that lump in my throat.

She was kicking back with her feet slung over the seat in front, filing her nails, which is not something most fifth graders do.

"How come you're so afraid to get into cars, anyway?" she said, out of the blue.

My stomach knotted up, as if she'd actually reached in there and given it a twist instead of just saying words. I saw that day flash in front my eyes before I could help it, heard Mom slam the front door shut, and then the car door too.

"What does that have to do with anything?" I said, bristling.

"Is it because of your mom?" she pressed, like she was trying to pick a fight. "It's not the car's fault she didn't come home, is it?"

"Cut it out!" I said, louder than I'd meant to. "Why can't you just be my friend!"

Sabrina sat bolt upright, dropping her hands in her lap. "I'm trying!" she said, and for a moment, her voice sounded just like mine, maybe because we were both so mad. "I'm trying to get you to face facts!" We stared at each other a moment longer, both furious, until she slouched down again and picked up her emery board. "It won't be for much longer anyway because we're moving. Dad's orders just came in. We're headed for Timbuktu."

"What?" I said, panic setting in. "What are you talking about? That's a lie." Who went to Timbuktu? I wasn't even sure it was a real place. But she just kept filing her nails, so I started babbling like some doppelganger had taken control of my mouth. "You can't go, Sabrina, you just can't," I said. "You can't because . . . because . . . I *need* you."

"Nope, you don't." She filed her nails real hard for a moment longer, like she was trying to stay mad, then gave it up and sighed, looking toward the stage. "Melanie, you know things haven't been good between us for a while."

I wasn't ashamed to beg. "I'll start listening to you, I promise I will. Please, Sabrina, I know you've been right about everything. I just had to . . . I just had to . . . *try*." I wanted to stop, but my mouth kept right on, and the next few words were like balls I was fumbling, trying to hang onto even as they tumbled out. "Besides, don't you know that it's been exactly one year since Mom left?"

And it was true, today was the anniversary, even though I'd tried to prevent it, just like the Grinch who couldn't stop Christmas. It wasn't my bad night in the window seat that was bugging me, it wasn't Karen or Leanne or the fact that Neverland had turned out to be nothing but a pile of dust, it was the fact that you can't stop some things from happening, no matter how hard you try.

"She's coming to opening night, you'll see!" I blurted, even though I couldn't see it anymore in my mind's eye, couldn't see anything but an empty seat where my mother was supposed to be.

Sabrina looked at me, then, and her eyes weren't sharp but glossy. They reminded me of that time when I was seven and had woken up in the middle of the night, feeling like I should look in the bathroom mirror, without knowing why. I had gazed into my own eyes, seeing all the flecks and the blackness of the pupils, knowing it was night all over the hemisphere and that everyone was asleep, until my eyes seemed like tunnels to my kooky seven-year-old mind, tunnels that went off into infinity.

It's hard to explain.

"You're going to be alright, Melanie," she said, and I wanted to believe her. "You're going to be just fine without me, you'll see. And you were right to try. You were right all along, about everything, can't you get that into your thick head?"

But it wasn't like she was insulting me, because we were both crying, her eyes all squinty, and mine with fat tears rolling out that I smeared away with the back of my hand. And I knew then that Sabrina and I were both more than friends and less, that we were the only two people in the world that really understood each other, and that all that secret-keeping didn't matter because of what was in our hearts. Miss Gorman walked on stage to call the cast together for another go, and I swear I only looked away for a split second, just long enough to see Karen watching me from the wings.

But when I looked back to Sabrina, she was gone.

"Melanie?" Miss Gorman said, turning in a circle, then spying me out in my seat. "Oh, there you are. Let's run the final scene, shall we?"

## TWENTY TWO
# The Final Cut

"Put up those swords, boys!" Miss Gorman cried. "Colin, Davis, remember the contract!"

Miss Gorman had gotten them to sign a behavioral contract a couple weeks back, but I was thinking she'd left out a few important clauses.

"Avast, look at me! I be on the poop deck!" Davis shouted, strutting around with one hand on his hip, waving his sword in the other.

"Blaggards and blasphemy!" Colin assumed a fencer's crouch. "'Tis me very *own* poop deck, and the poopiest deck it be in the history of mayhem and plunder!"

After that, it was a race to see how many times they could get the word poop into a sentence before Miss Gorman confiscated their weapons.

Barely enough time for me to pull myself together.

"What? Oh, *good*," Miss Gorman said with relief, turning around as I came up behind. She jammed a few loose strands of hair back into her pony tail. "Refresh my memory, Melanie. Are there any pirates in the last scene?"

I told her *no*, the last scene took place in the nursery.

"Of course, yes," she said, smiling now from ear to ear.

I tried to get into character as the backstage crew pushed the set around, wheeling out boulders and trees, dragging in the doll house and Wendy's bed. But I couldn't find my muse. It didn't help that Leanne stood a couple of feet behind me, sucking all the magic out of life with her *scribble, scribble.* That was the trouble with the theater arts. There was no avoiding people. And now Karen had come up alongside, flipping her hair over her knees to rub her fingers through it, like she was trying to roto-rooter out a drain.

"Ah, much better," she said as she whipped it back. "Don't you miss your old hair, Melanie? What's it feel like to be—oh, I mean, to *play* a boy."

I didn't say anything, just stared ahead, waiting for my cue.

"Hey Lee Lee, could you help me out with this clasp?" Karen lifted the hair off her neck, smiling my way as Leanne came up and fixed her nightie. "It's so nice to have friends around, don't you think?"

Luckily, Jeanette and Harry had almost finished their lines. When you mix Jeanette's blandness with Harry's stutter, it's like somebody slipped you a mickey. Everyone was getting snoozy.

I left Karen in the shadows and took my mark.

"Tink, where are you? Quick, close the window."

I was pretty sure it was Tammy, not Tory, doing my dirty work today, barring the window so that Wendy would think her mother had locked her out. There was a certain satisfaction in this plot twist, but unfortunately, Peter had to come to his senses.

"We can't both have her, lady!" I said, watching Jeanette moon over her lost child, but I don't think I got the intonation quite right, because I sounded like I worked in a diner. Then I had my change of heart and said, "Come on, Tink, we don't want any silly mothers."

I flew out the window, and Wendy took the stage. Actually, I didn't *fly*—Mr. Olford hadn't quite worked out the pulley system, though everyone said it would be up and running by opening night. I hoped to get a little practice in before then so that I didn't careen into the audience and land on some lady's lap.

The lump in my throat had shrunk, but it was still there, walnut-sized, and I pictured my little squirrel friends, pushing it past my larynx. I figured I could keep it together if I stayed in character, but stray thoughts of Leanne and Sabrina kept floating by, and then the sound of the car door slamming the last time I saw Mom.

"I see them in their beds so often in my dreams that I seem to see them when I am awake," Jeanette said, like she was reading a shopping list. "So often their silver voices call me, my little children whom I'll see no more."

It didn't matter that the acting was awful. By the time the reunion scene was underway, and Jeanette was hugging her wayward children one by one, my eyesight was all blurry, and the lump was growing. Then, the lost boys trooped in, looking for a handout because it seemed that moms were on sale that day—for everyone but me.

"Is your name Slightly?" Liza said to the lost-boy-in-chief.

"Yes'm," he said.

"Then I am your mother."

"How do you know?" he asked, which was at least a rational question.

"I feel it in my bones."

I was so messed up, I even missed my cue.

"Peter!" Wendy cried, and I gave a start.

I hurried onto the stage, mumbling my hellos while Wendy tried to get me to profess my love for her. Mr. Barrie had some strange ideas.

"Peter, where are you?" Jeanette said, spinning around as if she couldn't see me right in front of her face. "Let me adopt you too."

It was a stupid play, and I didn't know why I was letting it get to me. That was all I could think, standing there and forgetting my lines, what a stupid play it was, and how stupid I'd been to think there were doors in the world that led to stupid places like Neverland. It was the perfect name, after all, because it *wasn't* Everland and it *wasn't* Foreverland. It was a lonely, horrible place where you never saw your mother again, the place where Peter was doomed to live out his stupid life for all of time.

"Would you send me to school?" I sounded angry.

"Yes," Jeanette said with a motherly smile at the ceiling since she supposedly couldn't see me.

"And then to an office?"

Jeanette faltered, maybe because my voice was cracking.

"Um, I suppose so."

"Soon I should be a man?"

"Very soon," she said, and took a few steps back.

"I don't want to go to school and learn solemn things!" I yelled. "I want always to be a little boy and to have fun!" The lines were just as written, but I could feel all the oxygen go out of the room because of the way I was freaking everyone out.

Everyone but Karen.

"You will be rather lonely in the evenings, Peter," Wendy taunted, even though that line wasn't supposed to come until later.

"I shall have Tink," I said as the tears started to flow.

"You know Tink doesn't love ugly little boys," Karen said, and now she was totally off-script. "Nobody does." She took a few steps closer, because it was her nature, I guess, because blood was in the water and she couldn't resist. "Why don't you fly away, Peter, back to Neverland where you belong."

"Karen!" Miss Gorman cried, rushing up onto the stage with her notes spilling all around. "What on earth are you doing?"

But I didn't care anymore. The tears were coming so fast, I couldn't see anything at all—not Karen, not Miss Gorman, not Leanne looking on from her cloud castle while Karen tore me to bits. I was glad I couldn't see them, glad that I was alone because, all of a sudden, another door had opened, and I was getting sucked right through.

"I hate you!" I yelled, or it must have been me, even though I didn't recognize my voice. "I hate all of you!"

I was sorry the moment I said it because I couldn't take it back.

"Melanie, sweetheart," Miss Gorman was saying, and I could see her fixing to pat me all over, like the hurt could be dusted off, easy as one-two-three.

But I didn't want her either. The only person I wanted was the one I couldn't have. And even though I couldn't see, even though all those tears made the auditorium swim, I ran down the stairs, up the aisle, and out the double doors, headed for home.

## TWENTY THREE
# *Departure Times*

I was halfway home when I remembered my notebook.

It was still lying on the floor in the fifth row where I'd left it when Sabrina and I said our goodbyes. And I had an awful feeling about it as I stood there on First Avenue, frozen in place, as though I were in a horror movie and had just heard the gentleman with the axe help himself to some leftovers in the fridge.

I raced back.

If a person ever ran faster than I did that day, they should get written up in the Guinness Book of World Records. I ran through intersections with all the horns honking and people tossing their hands up behind the wheel, and I cut across lawns, and by the time I busted through those double doors into the auditorium, I was so out of breath, I had to bend over my knees.

It was dim in there, after the bright day, so it took a moment for me to see what was going on. Miss Gorman was nowhere to be seen, and the remains of the cast were sitting on the edge of the stage, or parked in the first row, or even kneeling behind Karen to look over her shoulder, because there she was in the middle of it all.

And I knew, like I'd been born knowing it, exactly what she was doing.

"Oh my God!" she cried, jiggling the journal around as she did a happy dance on her bottom. "She thinks houses have spirits! Listen to this: 'And sometimes, if you're quiet enough, they'll tell you their secrets, just like they've been waiting for you all those years with the whole world changing right outside their doors.' Oooh! Look at me, I'm the ghost of a house!" She made a spooky noise and floated the fingers of one hand up into the air.

I must have stopped breathing then. I felt the blood drain out of my body, and I thought for sure I was a goner because how could a person go on living after something like this? I'd heard of folks who dreamed they showed up at the office without any pants on, but this was worse, like I'd been stripped bare of all my clothes and my insides too, and everyone was gathered around, pointing and laughing at my scrawny little soul.

They were so caught up, no one even noticed me until I was right there, grabbing for the journal in Karen's hand.

"Hey!" she said, leaning back to dodge me, even as she kept on reading, because she'd flipped the page and didn't like what she saw. "I do *not* look like a mugger with a nylon pulled down over my face! You little creep!" But I must have hit the mark, because Colin and Davis lost it, keeling over backwards, and besides, it's factually true that Karen has a smushed-looking nose and droopy eyes, and that her hair is limp unless she roto-rooters it.

I snatched that journal right out of her hands and didn't say a word. I was full to the brim with feeling bad and didn't want to add any more regrets. Then, I saw Leanne, half hidden behind the curtains backstage with both hands clamped over her mouth.

"Oh, *Melanie*," Miss Gorman cried, rushing down the aisle, "I was so worried. I've been looking every— Melanie! Oh, please, Melanie, come back!"

I was nearly to the double doors when I heard Leanne, crying out in a voice so raw and loud, I hardly recognized it.

*"Mellllll!"* she cried, but I was already gone.

I burst through the front door at home to find myself smack in the middle of another big scene.

"Look at these!" Gloria was saying, shaking a pile of postcards under Dad's nose. "Just look at them! That's it, Mister I'll-Parent-Her-in-My-Own-Way. Undeliverable, the postmaster said. And he's been collecting these for weeks, just waiting for you to happen by. But *noooo*, Mister Big-Shot-Artist has better things to do!"

Dad was just staring at the handful of postcards, all tattered and bent now, after having been nowhere in a hurry, not at all as they'd been when I put them in the mailbox. His faun eyes were pulled together under his eyebrows, that's how worried he was, feeling awful because he was such a rotten dad and only thought about himself.

Right now, I didn't care.

"That's it," Gloria said again. "I'm calling Dr. Grossman first thing tomorrow morning!"

They didn't notice me any more than the kids at school. Then I saw that Dad's painting wasn't there, and I knew he'd sold it off without me even getting to say goodbye. The universe was gone with all its beautiful colors and swirls, gone as if it had never existed, and I could see that it was all for nothing—whole days Dad had spent poking his head into black holes, looking for something that wasn't there. Now, there was just a big, white rectangle where the painting had hung, dusty around the edges because no one bothered to clean since the day Mom slammed out the door.

"Stop fighting!" I yelled. "Just stop it!" But I guess I wasn't done making regrets, because I fixed Dad in my sights and let him have it with both barrels. "Don't you even know what day it is?" I knew perfectly well that he did because he'd made me Mickey Mouse pancakes for breakfast and had given me two long hugs before school. But I had to keep going, so I bunched up my hands at my sides and yelled, "And it's all your fault! If you hadn't gone and made Mom mad, she never would have gone away! I *hate* you!" I screamed like a maniac. "Go away and leave me alone!"

I went away instead and ran upstairs to my room. They must have taken me at my word because no one followed. Maybe Dad couldn't bring himself to face me, and Gloria probably figured there was no escape.

But she was wrong.

Everyone has a breaking point. I slammed around my room for a while, opening and closing drawers without even knowing what I was looking for, feeling trapped like there was no way out. How do you get out of yourself? I kept falling onto my bed like I might go to sleep with a vengeance, then hopping up to pace around and argue my point, probably because I felt bad about what I'd said. I pretended I was a lawyer in my head and made my case about how no one gave a hoot, getting madder and madder all the time.

All of a sudden, I knew what to do.

I rifled through my desk until I found my dog's-head change purse and pinched it open, pulling out all the cash that Gloria had given me on birthdays and Christmases. I'd been saving up for a new bike, but plans change.

I had to see Mom. It was time.

I went to the window and eased it open, craning my head out to look below. There was an old lattice attached to the house. I'd never tried to shimmy down it before because, frankly, it barely looked up to its day job, helping the wisteria take over the eaves. I eased my belly onto the sill, and I'll admit it was dicey, but with all that adrenalin coursing through my body, giving me nerves of steel and altering my chemical composition, I was light as air.

In a flash, I was down, wheeling my bike real slow through the side yard, then slinging my leg over to head for town.

I was pretty sure the Greyhound bus left at five.

# TWENTY FOUR
## *Last Call*

The Fairview Greyhound station is a little rough.

It sits on the corner of Second and Hawthorn, trying to pass as a forgotten place when it knows it's only pathetic. There's a big parking lot where the buses pull in right next to the one-story, glassed-in building, and people stand outside with duffel bags, smoking cigarettes all day, or going next door to Mickey's Diner for a cup of coffee.

I rode up on my bike and parked it in the rack at the diner, wishing I'd thought to bring my lock and chain. But there was nothing else to do, so I sent up a prayer to the saint of temporarily abandoned bicycles, even though I didn't know when I'd be back.

I wasn't thinking that far ahead.

The question in my mind now was how could I get a ticket? The man behind the counter wasn't going to sell me one without asking a lot of questions. I pulled open the door and scooted in, staying out of sight, which was easy with all those bedraggled customers hanging around, yelling at their toddlers or juggling bags, cigarettes hanging out of their mouths. There were vinyl chairs bolted to the floor all around the room, like maybe the Greyhound folks thought someone would steal them. They were mostly full, but I found an empty one in the corner and slipped in.

"Um, hello," I said to the man sitting next to me, slumped down with his elbows on the armrests and one of those old-fashioned fedoras pulled over his eyes. He popped it up and turned to look at me, wide-eyed. Maybe he wasn't used to people talking to him, what with that big, black beard taking over his face. He probably thought he was invisible.

"Hello," he said and just kept looking at me.

"Phew," I said, blowing out my cheeks, "I sure hope my folks get here soon. They're supposed to buy my ticket to go see my grandma, but I'm afraid they might be stuck at the hospital, looking after my brother, who's in a coma." It was an elaborate lie, but I was nervous.

He blinked a few times, so I knew he was still breathing.

“Do you think you could buy my ticket for me, in case they don’t show?” I pulled out my wad of cash, hoping he wouldn’t turn out to be a creep or a thief. What if the beard was a disguise and he was on the lam from the police for stealing some little girl’s dog’s-head change purse?

But I’d picked the right guy. Maybe he was a drifter and used to being pushed this way and that. He shrugged and took the cash as I told him where I was headed, then stood up to go get in line. It took about ten minutes for him to get up to the ticket seller, who was standing there like everything was a hassle, scratching his head with a pencil up under his visor while he listened to the bearded man place his order. My heart was thumping the whole time, but in the next minute he was back with my ticket and my change.

“You could keep that,” I said, nodding to the five-dollar bill in his hand, even though I was hoping he’d say no. Maybe he was a mind reader, in addition to being a mumbler, because I could barely hear what he said when he pushed the fiver back into my hand. Then he smiled under his beard, making all the stiff, black hairs shift around, and I felt something open up, way deep inside me, something I didn’t even know was clenched up like a fist.

“Last call!”

A man in a gray, button-up shirt and cap had come in through the side door and was yelling for people to board. He was hollering so loud I don't know how I missed it the first time.

"Thanks a lot," I said to the bearded man. I smiled hard to show how grateful I was, then hopped up and fell in with the folks who had answered the call, out the double glass doors and into the lot. The bus was fuming and rumbling, and already people were filing in, cramming their bags up the stairs before them, even though you're supposed to stow them down below. I guess people want all their loot with them, so when I got up to the aisle, I had to step over all sorts of things, guitars and backpacks and even somebody's potted plant. I went all the way to the back and smushed myself into a window seat.

I was so busy hoping no one would sit beside me, I hardly thought about the fact that in a few minutes, we'd be driving. But people kept filing in, so I switched to hoping that whoever it was wouldn't smell like cigarettes or have booze on their breath. Maybe some little old lady would be going off to see her niece.

"Can I sit here?"

It was a teenager, a deeply suspicious category of humanity.

"Sure," I peeped.

The boy somehow wedged his skinny legs under the seat in front and got down as low as he could, like a jack-in-the-box, ready to spring.

"You taking the bus by yourself?" I said. When I'm nervous, I say all sorts of stupid things.

He said *duh* at me with his eyes, then closed them and managed to slouch down another inch or two, compressing his spine with some teenage superpower that should be discoverable by medical science with the right kind of tools.

This was almost as good as having a grandma beside me, because during the whole trip, he didn't say a word. Maybe my drive with Gloria had helped, or maybe I was too worn out to be scared anymore. I stared out at the telephone poles flicking by, strung together by wires that looped down and up, down and up, until I thought I was going into a hypnotic trance. There were itty-bitty towns scattered along the road that you might miss if you blinked, just a gas station and a grocery store and maybe a seedy motel that couldn't be forgotten because no one had ever noticed it in the first place.

I got drowsy with the hum of wheels on the pavement, and before I knew it, the driver was shaking my shoulder.

"Grayson," he said, as if that was the only word he knew.

I looked out at the one-story glassed-in bus station with a diner next door, just like back in Fairview. It was like I'd woken up inside one of those dreams where you keep running but never get anywhere. But then, my eyes roamed on to the century courthouse and the five-and-dime, and it all came flooding back along with a crowd of memories, walking around like ghosts, arm in arm.

Maybe it had been easier, thinking Mom was off in some big city I'd hardly ever seen.

"Oh, thanks," I said, and hustled down the aisle, glad that I was traveling light. When I stepped out, the air smelled different, even though Grayson is only about fifty miles from Fairview. I took in a deep breath, feeling so happy-sad I could hardly get it past the lump in my throat.

I knew where I was headed, so I didn't waste any time. Downtown Grayson looks a lot like Fairview, twins separated at birth. Maybe one of them is the doppelganger of the other, but I couldn't say which is real. Fairview seems like the imposter sometimes because it's so new, to me at any rate, and Grayson because it's so old, populated by all those ghosts weaving in and out among the regular people. I passed the coffee shop that Mom always took me to for a treat, and the Grayson library, which almost had me balling. I guess you never forget your first library card.

After a few turns, I was headed to the outskirts of town. I didn't want to go by my old house. It was already getting dusky, and I thought if I saw it, I might break down completely, like a car whose wheels had come right off and rolled away. Then, I'd never get to where I needed to be. Part of me was wishing I could go home, my old home, that is, but I knew it was a ghost house now, waiting for someone else to tell its secrets to. That was sad, that our time was past, and that all those memories didn't belong to me anymore, except maybe as postcards I had sent myself with a bung address, all scratched up and tattered.

I turned down Franklin, then Madison, then Taylor, and when I was out of presidents, I had finally arrived. Full dusk had settled in, and the shadows were long across the hillside, casting little pools of darkness behind the gravestones. I looked up at the sign, arching over the wide, gravel drive.

ELMWOOD CEMETERY, the sign read, WHERE SOULS COME HOME TO REST.

# TWENTY FIVE
# *Falling*

The moment I read that sign, I was lost to the world.

I ran under the arch, stumbling and then scrambling up as if the weeds were catching at my legs, as if they were the arms of corpses, pulling me down. The whole time, I was crying, searching those gravestones, one by one, because I'd never been here before, not even for the funeral that everyone had attended but me. I hadn't wanted to see that slab of granite standing over what used to be my mother, because stone is stone, and it can't feel and it can't love, and it doesn't make you breakfast for dinner because that's your favorite thing to eat. I hadn't wanted to see that tombstone with the most precious name in the world etched into it.

Lydia Harper.

I fell to my knees in front of it. It looked exactly as I had imagined it, white and cold with dates etched beneath her name, and words that read, *wife, daughter, mother, friend to the lonely, poet to the world.* I didn't know who had come up with that, but it was exactly her, my mom boiled down to eleven little words, like a message from the other side. I started pawing at the ground, getting dirt under my fingernails until it hurt, only I wasn't getting anywhere, so I tore up grass and flowers instead, bundling them into my arms, not thinking at all but just needing to get down as close as I could.

"Mommy!" I cried, even though I hadn't called her that in years. "Mommmmmy!" And the louder and longer I called for her, the more the sound echoed down inside me, because I knew now I had fallen all the way in. The abyss had been there all along, a bottomless pit falling away on every side as I went through my day, skirting up to the edge with my head in the clouds, not even noticing I was inches away from never landing. But I'd fallen now, and I knew this was the real thing, and that everything before was just child's play.

"Moo Moo!"

I could barely hear the words over my own sobs, when all of a sudden, there was Dad, down in the dirt, crushing me into his arms.

I fell into him like he was the abyss.

"I can't, I can't," I cried, hugging him all over his body and clutching his shirt like maybe if I got close enough, I could crawl inside. I was hitting him too, even as I hung on, hitting him on his arms and chest with my fists all balled up. And the whole time, he just said, "Moo Moo, my baby," over and over, crying his eyes out as he kissed my hair.

But after a while, even the saddest person in the world can't cry any more.

That's what happened to us. I knew I was still falling, but it was different now, not plummeting, just slow and weightless and dark. We sat there, collapsed into each other with me half in his lap, my arms flung around his shoulders and my cheek against his heaving chest. He was holding on so tight I could hardly breathe, especially being so ragged from all those sobs, but I didn't care. I wouldn't ever let go.

Then I saw Sabrina, coming up over the hill, out beyond the gravestones.

I eased back and smeared a hand across each eye.

"Dad," I said, all hiccuppy, "could I have a moment alone?"

He looked me hard in the face, but I guess he must have seen it was alright, because he kissed my cheek, leaving his lips there for a long time, then got up and dusted himself off.

"I'll be out by the car," he said, his voice husky like I'd never heard it before.

***

"I didn't think I'd ever see you again," I said, trying to get control over my voice.

"Don't be such a dummy," she said, already looking less like Charlie's smartest angel and more like me that day in the mirror when I was seven years old. Maybe that's when the idea was born, even though I didn't know it at the time, just felt an inkling of the infinity inside.

Sabrina was my best invention.

"I thought sending myself those postcards from Mom would make me feel closer to her," I said, "but it only made things worse. I can't believe I'm never going to see her again." I started to plummet again, because I couldn't get my mind around the idea that she was gone, it was so deep and wide, and I thought maybe that's what the abyss was—an unfathomable eternity without the person I loved best. It was a Neverland, but not of my own making.

"You don't fall forever," Sabrina-who-was-me said. "If you let go, you come out the other side. The thing is to not get stuck, up there on the edge, thinking there's no way out."

I realized there were things Sabrina knew that I did not, which was wonderful and strange since I'd made her up in the first place, and she was only and always an imaginary friend.

"I take exception to the *only* part," she said with a smile, and then we both started laughing, with a little left-over crying thrown in for good measure.

"I never could have done it without you!" I said. "None of it!" Then, I asked something I'd been wondering about. "But how come you showed up when you did? Was it Karen?" I guessed, because it occurred to me that in my old life, I might never have stood up to her.

She quirked her wouldn't-you-like-to-know smile, then said, "Well, I never could resist an anniversary."

Of course, I'd known all along I was playing a big game of make-believe, but aren't we all? At least I know it, which is more than I can say for most people. And I guess, looking back, that I did it on purpose, because I *could*, because I needed a friend. Maybe Sabrina-who-was-me had wanted me to fall into the abyss the whole time just so I could fall out the other side someday.

"Do you think she misses her body?" I said, thinking about Mom floating up above the mangled car that was flipped over in the ditch. The officer's report had said there was nothing she could do, so I knew it wasn't Dad's fault, no matter what I'd said.

It wasn't that she was mad and driving like a loony, just because she thought Dad was trying to talk her out of her dreams. The oncoming car had crossed the line all on its own, and there was no getting out of it. "Do you think she tried to stay?" I said, which is what I really wanted to know.

"I'm sure she held on as long as she could," Sabrina said, and I felt like she knew, what with having come out of the infinity inside me. Who knows, maybe she met Mom passing through. "And when she let go, it was like doves fluttering out of her fingers and her mouth," she said, and now she didn't look like Sabrina Duncan at all, and not even like me, but like my beautiful mother with her long, dark hair and her eyes full of stars.

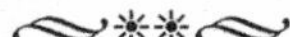

I went back to the car after we'd said our last goodbyes, but I could tell Sabrina was still there, somewhere inside.

"Criminy, child, you gave us a heart attack!" Gloria said, sliding her rear off the hood of the Nova and crushing her cigarette into the ground with her heel. Gloria is a terrible litter bug. "Don't ever do that again, you hear?"

I thought about her driving Dad all this way, barreling around corners and probably running lights, cursing the fuzz all the way. She had lots of nicknames for law enforcement officials, trying to get even with them for having all that clout.

I took Dad's hand in my own, looking to see if the knuckles were still white from hanging on for dear life. Then I folded it up and kissed it, smiling up at him, thinking I'd better take good care of him, and maybe Gloria too.

We were all we had.

"Come on, I'll take you both out to ice cream," Gloria said, and we all piled into the car.

## TWENTY SIX
# *Gossamer and Monkey-do*

I knew I'd have to go back to school someday. Monday, in fact. Dad had let me stay home Friday and lie around the house all weekend, just like I was sick without the germs. I guess word had gotten around about me running off, and when people feel guilty they'll let you do all kinds of things.

But eventually, we all have to face the music.

I've always wondered about that idiom. What kind of music is it, and why is it so awful? Maybe it's loud enough to blast your hair off as it comes out of speakers fifty feet high. I tend to think it's organ music, which is something sane people only agree to listen to when they're in church, parked on some hard, uncomfortable pew, waiting for the minister to come out and tell them about what terrible people they are.

But, I digress.

"Melanie, it's so lovely to see you," Miss Gorman gushed, as if I'd been gone a month. That was embarrassing but still nice to hear, and I could tell she meant it because her eyes got misty. "Come here, sweetie," she said, and pulled me in for a hug, right there by the doorway with everyone filing past to go to their desks.

"Thanks, Miss Gorman," I said, and then she schooled me about her name again when we both knew I was never going to call her Laurelann. Speaking of idioms, I'll just say this: a tiger never changes its stripes.

I'd gotten through the day okay without looking at Leanne once, even though I could feel her watching me the whole time. I felt bad about that, but I couldn't bring myself to meet her eyes, thinking it would only remind me about all those times she'd just stood by while Karen dumped loads of monkey-do all over my reputation. Maybe Leanne was sorry, I don't know, but it was a little late for that.

And speaking of Karen, she'd been all flowers and butterflies that day, probably because she'd gotten a serious talking-to by Miss Gorman and the other people in charge. You can't go around dumping loads of monkey-do on other folks without it eventually coming around, and I was pretty sure she'd had her own load to deal with that weekend. But she'd be back to her old ways in no time. I didn't really care one way or the other, because I was done with pussyfooting around, letting other people tell me who I was.

And that's when I suspected Sabrina wasn't gone at all but had moved in to stay.

"Class, I've had a special request," Miss Gorman said when we were all settled at our desks. "Leanne has written a paper that she'd like to share with the class."

That got my attention. Leanne never shared her papers with the class, even when it was required. Miss Gorman bends the rules all the time, just so no one will get conked on the head. Leanne was already getting to her feet and shuffling up to the front of the room, her face as white as the paper that was shaking in her hands. All of a sudden, I felt sorry for her, thinking I never knew how terrified she must be all of the time.

"My essay," she began, her voice shaking, just like the paper. "My essay," she tried again, "is about my best friend, Melanie Harper."

My mouth dropped open for the whole class to see.

"Melanie isn't like anyone I know," Leanne said, looking down at the page. "She is the kind of fearless person I have always wanted to be. She knows more about the world than anyone I have ever met."

I didn't know the person she was talking about. In fact, I was thinking this was a person I would like to get better acquainted with.

"She's taught me all sorts of things, like how to hear the souls of houses talk to you and how to see diamonds in a pile of broken glass." She raised her eyes to mine, although they looked kind of swimmy to me, along with the rest of the room. "And she taught me that a real friend doesn't go around only thinking about herself, even if that's all she was used to thinking about before."

Leanne's voice had been getting stronger as she talked, but when she got to this part, all of a sudden she started balling, only silently, with the tears streaming out of her eyes. I didn't know how she could keep on talking, but she did, right through the tiny hiccups and all those tears.

"I wish I had known her all my life, because then maybe it wouldn't have taken me so long to be a better friend. I know I'll never be fearless, but at least I can be brave, because who wants to go through life if there isn't anybody to share it with? Melanie taught me that too, because before I met her, I was all alone up there in the clouds. But then, she came and got me."

I couldn't believe she was fessing up about cloud castles and the souls of houses when she must have known it was all going into Karen's next load of monkey-do. It was like she'd opened her own notebook for everyone to see—and then I understood that was exactly what she'd done, stripped her own insides bare so that it wasn't just me up there before the school, but her too.

I think Leanne must be the best friend in the whole world.

Neither one of us could keep it together, what with her going on and on about pixie dust and happy endings that you had to make up yourself. I felt like I was seeing parts of Leanne's soul I'd never noticed before, and it was different than mine, soft and filmy, like the pearly inside of a shell, or like gossamer you had to handle carefully so it wouldn't tear. She sat down at her desk again, and then Miss Gorman went on with the class, so it wasn't until the bell rang that we had a chance to talk.

We both sat at our desks until most of the kids were gone. I wasn't sure which one of us would have the nerve to move first, but I guess she was trying out her new habit of being brave because when I looked up, she was standing before my desk, just like that first day when she'd asked for my help.

"I'm so sorry, Mel," she breathed, barely getting out the words. "I wanted to stand up for you that whole time, really, I did. And I wanted to tell Karen how mean she was being, only I was afraid that I—afraid that I—" And then she dropped off as if she didn't know exactly what she'd been afraid of.

It didn't matter though. I knew what she meant. And as it turned out, she had even put Miss Gorman up to asking for my help writing her paper, that first, fateful day.

"I just wanted to be friends!" she said, and that started us crying all over again, only now we were smiling too, so wide it hurt.

"Hey, Melanie," Colin cried out from the back of the classroom where he and Davis were killing time until play practice, twisting tinfoil sheets into antennae hats, probably for the purpose of detecting alien lifeforms. It was clear he had no idea what was going on between Leanne and me. Colin lives in a two-person universe, even though everyone else is invited to stop by. "Do you have anything else in your journal about Karen?" he said. "That part about the mugger was really funny."

I didn't feel as good about that as I might have a few days ago, now that I was getting used to taking care of myself out loud.

"Nope," I lied, "but maybe later we can play a game I made up. It's called when-the-soul-of-a-house-goes-*bad*."

"Cooooool," Colin and Davis said together, then put on their hats.

## TWENTY SEVEN
# *Hiding in Plain Sight*

I think the whole town of Fairview turned out for the opening night of *Peter Pan*, and half of Grayson too. Gloria had strolled around the greater Clarkson County region in her velour sweat suit, handing out posters and being persuasive as only a woman wearing gold lamé tennies can be.

"Break a leg!" she yelled from the front row as I peeked around the curtain. She was sitting beside Dad, who was decked out in one of Roland's wool blazers, looking handsome with his faun eyes shining and a faint smile on his face.

I wondered if Miss Gorman would notice.

And, speaking of Roland, he and Roxie were there too, and lots of people from my old neighborhood in Grayson. I even saw Leanne's parents a few rows back, looking like they'd just popped in from the country club to see how the other half lived. Only they were smiling and laughing with the old, ratty couple sitting next to them, so I must have gotten them wrong too.

I was feeling so good, I decided I might even talk to Gloria's shrink, Mr. Grossman, when this was all over. I knew now what Roland meant when he said you have to choose, even if you only have one option.

My beautiful mother was gone.

How could I choose that? I was never going to see her soft, shining eyes, not ever again. I'd never smell her cozy, lived-in smell as we cuddled in the window seat, never feel her lips on my cheek as she leaned over my bed, never hear her say my name.

Melanie.

But how could I *not* choose it? Because as long as I was missing her, she was gone from my heart too. So I had to try, even though I didn't know how. And I figured, what the heck, between the shrink and Dad and Gloria, with Roland and Roxie cheering me on from the ranks and Leanne by my side, maybe I could learn to let go.

Actors are a superstitious lot, so I shook off Gloria's dubious pep talk as I ducked back behind the curtain. I know that *break a leg* is just an idiom, and that no one really wants you to end up in traction, but after all, I was going to be spreading my wings for the first time that night. Mr. Olford had finally worked out the pulley system, just an hour before the show.

"Remember, Mel, lift off slowly," Leanne said, walking up with her clipboard smashed against her chest. She was a mess, all loaded up with the pressure of managing a major theatrical production. But she kept her head, dishing out orders to the set crew and keeping everyone in line, even Colin and Davis, whom she bribed with pop rocks. "Don't go bouncing off, Mel, because the suspension system is really tight."

I wasn't sure what that meant because science isn't my strong suit. But I reassured her as best I could, prying her hand off her clipboard to give it a squeeze.

I guess I should tell you about Karen too. She strutted around backstage, flipping her head over every two minutes, even though Wendy isn't supposed to have feathered hair. You can't put lipstick on a pig, but that doesn't stop a few pigs from trying. Kim helped her out, hopping around in her mermaid tail, getting her fingers into Karen's hair like she was giving her a shampoo. But Karen must not have liked that, because she put on one of her bug-eyed looks that Kim doesn't understand. I think if Karen is ever going to get anywhere with Kim, she'll have to resort to stronger tactics, maybe squirting her with a mild vinegar solution like you do when you're house-training a dog.

Finally, the audience quieted to a hush, and the curtain rose on Cory Plath, lying on the nursery rug in his role as Nana, dog-turned-nursemaid. He romped around on all fours, playing house and getting the children ready for bed, which earned a big laugh from the audience. It's not hard to charm a willing crowd, and Cory was romping for all he was worth. Then came the scene with the elder Darlings, tucking their children into bed and heading off to the theater. Before I knew it, I was crouched right there on the window sill.

I don't know what was different this time. Maybe Mom really was there, after all, watching from on high or from inside or wherever it is heaven hides. Maybe it was the audience, helping me with all their imaginations joined together like a magic spotlight, but there was no door to pass through this time. I was just *there*, in Victorian England in all its mysterious, old-fashioned splendor. I wondered whether I should just leave the Darlings to live out their ordinary lives because Neverland was equal parts wonder and longing, and that kind of thing changes a person forever. But then, that's the nature of magic, even if science hasn't discovered it yet.

So off we went.

Or off *I* went.

Bounding, as I was counseled not to do, and swinging out over the audience on a wire attached to my bum.

"I can fly! Look, Wendy, I can fly!" I ad-libbed, trying to pretend I was just showing off and wasn't in a state of mortal terror. And if my voice squeaked a little, the audience must have thought it was part of the role, because they roared out with wonder and delight. I had a close call as I grazed some lady's hairdo, but then I was back over the stage on terra firma, landing with a few stumbles that were quickly forgiven.

Like I said, it was an easy crowd.

The rest of the play went off without a hitch. There's something about being together in the moment that brings out the best in people, so we had them laughing and crying and throwing an arm around the shoulder of the person sitting next door. Once, I caught Leanne's eye as she stood beaming in the shadows, like a mother hen whose eggs had all hatched at once.

And maybe I got sprinkled with pixie dust, because all of a sudden I knew that the real and the pretend weren't separate at all. One wasn't better than the other, because they were always shining *through* each other, like prisms, and that's what made my pile of junky old glass shimmer like jewels. Heaven was hiding in plain sight, only you had to know something before you could see it, a secret as simple as the one that made pixie dust glow.

And the secret was this: anything is possible, if only you *believe*.

## ACKNOWLEDGMENTS

I'll let you in on a little secret. Aspiring authors spend long hours drafting (in their heads) the acknowledgments pages of their yet-to-be-released, forthcoming instant classics. It makes a nice change from crafting the acceptance speech for (insert your favorite award) — in my case the Newberry, with maybe a Hugo and an Edgar thrown in for good measure (and who would say *no* to a National Book Award, a Pulitzer or, heck, a Nobel Prize in Literature?). By mentioning these accolades, I'm hoping to confuse some of you into thinking I've actually won them. Let me know how that goes.

But this page isn't about me, it's about the people who supported me on my writing journey. I'll start with my parents, Dan and Mary, who read countless drafts of the *countless* novels I wrote while I was pursuing my craft. They offered encouragement, advice, praise, and a shoulder to cry on when needed.

My husband, Johnny, was my rock and my beacon. Sorry to offend with such a shameless cliché, but in Johnny's case, it's true. He had faith in my dream when mine was shaken, he made me laugh, and he paid the bills. Thanks, honey.

My children, Jacob and Sophia, gave me the gift of listening, over the years, as I read them many of the aforementioned Newberrys, most of the classics I loved as a child, and finally, my very own books. They said they loved them, and I think they meant it. They also occasionally did the dishes and fed the goats without being asked. Mostly, I'm grateful to them for making me a mother, just by being born.

As for dear friends who have supported my writing, I am sure to forget to name too many of them. But I'll start with the five that come to mind immediately: Dan Dowhower, Rick Settersten, Pat Armstrong, Kimberly Gifford and Liddy Detar. Thanks for caring.

Thank you to Margaret Anderson, author extraordinaire, for her wonderful advice, and to my other talented beta-readers, Posie Farrand, Kylie Tully, Harper Hamblin, Amy Derby and Lynette Gottlieb. My former agent, Thao Le, was also an indispensable support with her enthusiasm, input and guidance. My copy editor, Nevin May, was thorough, patient, and a pleasure to work with, and my cover designer, Robin Vuchnich was equally kind — and talented.

And where would I be without my writing group? Thank you for all the Thursday nights, snacking on goodies, sipping tea, and listening to each other read and share. The arc of a writing life is long, but the journey is its own reward, and I'm glad to have shared the road with all of you.

Lastly, thanks to everyone who picks up this book. I hope you enjoy reading it as much as I did creating it.

Julie Mathison has been writing for 30 years, as a student of literature, a lawyer, and an avid creator of all things fictional, be they literary short stories or books for children. She lives on a farm in Corvallis, Oregon with her husband and two children, four goats, six sheep, one dog and more chickens than you can shake a stick at (literally – she has tried). She enjoys ambitious and tedious undertakings like running marathons, making jam, homeschooling her children, making jam, writing novels, and making jam.

Visit her at www.juliemathison.com